Sadie ROCKS!

SMILE!
IT'S MEANT TO BE FUN

D1331853

KAREN McCOMBIE

■SCHOLASTIC

For Faye Wylie
Thanks for coming along on the ride!

First published in the UK in 2009 by Scholastic Children's Books
An imprint of Scholastic Ltd
Euston House, 24 Eversholt Street
London, NW1 1DB, UK
Registered office: Westfield Road, Southam, Warwickshire, CV47 0RA
SCHOLASTIC and associated logos are trademarks and/or
registered trademarks of Scholastic Inc.

ISBN 978 1407 10784 4

A CIP catalogue record for this book is
available from the British Library.

Typeset by M Rules.
Printed in the UK by CPI Bookmarque, Croydon, Surrey.
Papers used by Scholastic Children's Books are made from
wood grown in sustainable forests.

3 5 7 9 10 8 6 4 2

www.scholastic.co.uk/zone

SMILE!
IT'S MEANT TO BE FUN

A big hello (and, I guess, so long). . .

. . .to the final instalment of Sadie Rocks! In this fourth book in the series, Sadie's twin brother's (awful) boy band are poised on the brink of pop superstardom. Though Sonny and the lads aren't exactly thrilled about a rival (nearly as awful) boy band who are trying to beat them to the top of the charts. Back in the (relatively) sane world of home, there're thrills, spills and some big surprises and shocks ready to rock Sadie's world. Hope you enjoy the ride with Sadie as much as I enjoyed writing it!

Mucho love,

Karen McCombie

Contents

1 Yabberers, and how to avoid them   1

2 The joy of the Trash Pad   15

3 Romeo and, er, Nicola. . .   28

4 My brother, the nerk   41

5 Every size of black cloud. . .   49

6 Weird, in the circumstances   60

7 Welcome to shopping hell   72

8 Sadie's Socks   85

9 Memories of meringues. . .   97

10 When instincts go wrong   107

11 Mission Detract Claws   112

12 The non-scientific experiment   119

13 Stare-offs and stressing   130

14 The sludge of gloom   139

15 Memories in *italics*   152

16 Whatever-itis   162

17 The significant something   173

18 Amazing, yet possibly *terrible*. . .   183

Yabberers, and how to avoid them

"It's true!"

"It *isn't*!"

"It is!"

"Nuh-*uh*, it isn't!"

"It is!!"

"Uh-uh. No way."

Y'know, I get bored easily.

It's not a fantastic personality trait, I know. I have some nice ones (I think), and I guess getting bored easily is better than being mean to little animals or being a compulsive liar or a serial killer or something.

But whatever; right now I was bored. Bored of the annoying *yabbering* going on behind me in the living room.

I gently wiggled the TV remote control out from under Clyde, our house rabbit, who gave a cute, surprised squeak, blinked his huge, long-lashed bunny eyes – and then bit me. (It's pretty

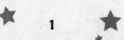

nice having a rabbit hopping about the house. It's just a pity that Clyde's worst personality trait is being mean to humans who dare to wake him up when he's snoozing.)

"Yeah!!"

"No WAY!!"

"*Definitely!!*"

Sigh. . .

That was yet *more* yabbering, coming from the direction of the sofa.

I shuffled closer across the carpet towards the TV. Not just to get away from the yabbering, but to be in with a chance of actually *seeing* anything on the TV, since it was the size of a cereal box. One of those weeny "fun-size" cereal boxes you get cellophaned together with a bunch of other midget-size boxes in variety packs. (Well, *practically* that small. And yeah, so exaggerating might be another of my not-so-hot personality traits.)

"No WAY!!"

"Yeah! Check it out!"

"Uh-*UH*!!"

I gritted my teeth and pressed the on button.

Ping! I pressed a random couple of digits on the remote and found myself at a shopping channel.

Great – I *loved* watching shopping channels.

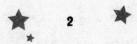

Not because I had a deep longing to own any of the dumb stuff they sold on there, but because I was fascinated by the amazing talents of the presenters, and their ability to witter on endlessly about how truly incredible the truly dumb stuff was.

"...*this genuine diamondesque, oval-cut piece of, well, art, has a stunning intensity about it, and could grace, well, any one of your fingers!!*"

(Translation: it's a ring.)

"...*and look at this! Wow! Isn't that an absolutely exquisite presentation?!*"

(Translation: it's in a box.)

"Like, *yeah*, it's true!" That wasn't a shopping-channel presenter. That was Yabberer No. 1, my twin brother, Sonny.

"You're MAD!!" That was Yabberer No. 2, his best mate, Kennedy.

"No, I'm not. I'm just *saying*. OK?" Sonny muttered, sounding sort of apologetic.

"But HOW can you say that?!" Kennedy gasped, sounding outraged.

It was no use. No matter how much I tried to bust my boredom by watching telly, the yabbering was going to win out.

How I wished that my almost-stepdad, Will, wasn't madly hoovering upstairs, so that maybe the

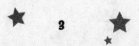

yabbering could go on in Sonny's room instead of on the sofa.

"Well, 'cause I *can*!" said Sonny.

"Wait a minute – so you're saying that HE'S better-looking than ME?" gasped Kennedy.

For a boy with a face like a plate, Kennedy really, really fancied himself.

I turned around and saw Sonny – holding a magazine open in his hands – shrug his shoulders. "But look . . . he *is* kind of cute!"

Now, it's not every day that you expect your thirteen-year-old brother to come out with a comment like that. But Sonny wasn't flicking through *Girls Like Us!* magazine and comparing the cuteness factor of singers for his own personal enjoyment.

Oh, no.

This was war.

Boy-Band War. . .

"Hey, what do YOU think, Sadie?" Kennedy yabbered some more, snatching the magazine from Sonny and holding it up, so a full-page poster of a fabulously furry guinea pig was cheek-to-cheek with his, er, cheeks.

"Wrong page," I droned, and Kennedy – never the smartest plate-faced boy on the planet – quickly flipped a page forward and resumed his

pose, now comparing his head to that of an ultra-handsome boy in a baseball cap, who looked maybe about fourteen or fifteen.

"See, Sadie? Cute – right?" said Sonny, pointing to the ultra-handsome face, trying to prove his point.

OK, I need to say right here, right now, that my stage-school-brat brother and a bunch of his stage-school-brat mates had somehow managed to land a real live contract with a real live record company. (Before anyone gets all impressed, I have to *also* say that it wasn't as remotely cool as it might sound. It was deeply corny. Their outfits were deeply corny, their dance routines were deeply corny and their songs were *brilliant*. Only joking! They were deeply corny too.)

The band even had their own mad stalker mega-fan (Mel) – or at least they *used to*, till our own mad grandmother shooed her away from outside our house not so long ago.

But here's the most important thing: the bratty stage-school band's first real live single was coming out in eleven days' time, and something had gone *badly* wrong in their plan for world domination. (Er, by that I mean of course the world of little kids and grannies, 'cause even though Sonny would never admit it, *that* was the

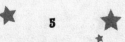

target audience for a cutesy junior boy band like his.)

And here's what had gone wrong: The Twist, a *rival* boy band. . .

It had all come out today. Hal – one of the other lads in Sonny's band – had brought his fourteen-year-old sister's magazine into the stage school and flashed around the article about The Twist. Sonny, Kennedy, Marcus, Hal and Ziggy were so incensed that it was a wonder *Girls Like Us!* magazine hadn't been ripped into tiny pieces and set on fire.

So, here I was: bored, and being forced into giving my opinion on whether Kennedy and his plate face was cuter than the boy in the photo (hey, Kennedy Watson would have to wait a *long* time – like slightly longer than for ever – to hear *me* call him cute).

Uh-oh, I'd just noticed that the boy in the photo – according to what was printed under his hundred-watt grin – was called *Benjii*, for goodness' sake. . .

"That's a *dog's* name, isn't it?!" I said with a shudder. "I mean, calling your band The Twits is bad enough!"

My rubbish yet semi-funny joke got Sonny semi-smiling, but Kennedy was frowning like he didn't get it.

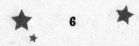

"They're called The *Twist*, Sadie! Not The *Twits*," he corrected me, the big idiot.

At least Sonny had the sense to roll his eyes at his best friend.

Speaking of jokes, my brother's band was called (get this) "Sadie Rocks". Which was a joke in itself, or at least using "Sadie" had started out that way. If I'd thought that Sonny and the other boys were seriously going to use it, I'd have changed my name from Sadie Bird to something far less embarrassing, like Brangelina Bob Sidebottom.

"Y'know, maybe I should've called myself Kennii, with two 'I's. . ." Kennedy added thoughtfully, or at least as thoughtfully as someone with two brain cells can manage.

The bosses at the stage school were to blame for suggesting he switched from Kenneth (which was on his birth certificate) to Kennedy (which was plain pretentious). Just like they'd suggested Alan should be Hal, Mark should be Marcus, and Gordon should become Ziggy. They seemed to think that Sonny was groovy enough as it was. (Please . . . don't give him *another* reason to be big-headed.)

"What's this?" asked a sing-song voice from the living-room doorway. It belonged to one of my grandmothers. Not the sane one, unfortunately.

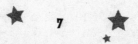

"You boys aren't still fretting over this other band, are you?"

This grandmother was Nonna (Italian for "granny", though she was about as Italian as Clyde, my rabbit). *This* grandmother was getting building work done on her retirement home in Spain, and was staying with us temporarily. She was driving my entire family mad, possibly permanently.

Ever since Nonna had arrived a few weeks ago, my mum had been bashing her most angry-sounding classical favourites out on the piano (imagining every key was Nonna's head, I suspected). What's more, my stepdad Will's slight obsessive-compulsive tendencies were becoming more obvious (though maybe he was just doing extra housework – and extra-*meticulous* housework – to keep himself out of Nonna's way). And Gran (my sensibly named Irish grandmother) had taken to phoning up first, so she could time her visits for when Nonna was off swanning around the art galleries of London.

The only two members of my family who got along with Nonna were a) Sonny, mainly because Nonna was completely starstruck by her talented grandson, and b) Martha, but I think that had a lot to do with the fact that babies like spangly things, and Nonna liked a bit of older lady bling.

"But, Nonna, it says here that The Twist's single is coming out this week!" whined Sonny, pointing at the feature on the other side of the page from Benjii's sugar-coated smile. "*And* they've got publicity in this magazine. Where does that leave us?"

Nonna breezed over to the sofa, her shortish, immaculately styled, silvery-gold hair glinting as much as her pearly pink loose-wrap cardie. She had on a huge necklace made out of a whole pinky-white shell. I wondered what kind it was, but there was no point asking her. Knowing Nonna, she'd instantly make up a whole new type of shell, previously unknown to marine biologists, and swear blind that it was for real.

"Sonny, I'm *sure* there's room for both your bands in the charts," Nonna murmured soothingly, putting on the glasses that had been dangling around her neck on a gold chain, clanking up against the shell pendant as she walked. "And, boys, you really *should* smile! It's meant to be fun!"

Actually, what Nonna said made sense (amazingly). I mean, *I* might think singing deeply corny songs and doing even cornier dance routines was horribly naff, but it was supposed to be what Sonny and his mates really wanted to do.

At Nonna's words, Sonny and Kennedy looked at each other and shrugged, trying a slight smile on for size. Not that it lasted long.

"So anyway, *this* one is the lead singer, same as *you*, Kennedy?" asked Nonna, studying first the band photo on one page, and Benjii's mug on the other.

"Yeah." Kennedy nodded, hands gripping the pages of the magazine tightly, as if he'd like to squash Benjii's head just as hard.

"Hmm . . . actually, I see what you mean now! This boy does have a *very* appealing smile. And *beautiful* eyes. The girls will certainly adore him!"

Her clunky words splattered over Kennedy like a bucket of ice-cold gloop.

"You've certainly got some competition there!" Nonna laughed blithely.

I liked Kennedy about as much as I liked a) Sonny's boy band, and b) Nonna staying in my bedroom (i.e., not a lot), but it wasn't exactly fun watching her destroy his and Sonny's dreams in one fell swoop of tactlessness. I wasn't *that* bored, *or* mean.

Plus, when Nonna was in full swing, she was just as likely to casually toss a tactless, cutting remark to anyone else unfortunate enough to be within range.

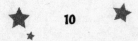

I was *out* of here.

"Got some homework to do. . ." I mumbled, jumping to my feet and scooping Clyde up with me.

My favourite secret(ish) hideout is the clump of trees down at the end of the garden. One wiggle through the bent railings and I'd be in the shrubbery, settling down in the spot under my pet Christmas tree (I'll explain later) and staring out at the old, rambling Victorian cemetery that our house backs on to.

But I wouldn't be going there today, since it was drizzling and grey outside, which pretty much matched the drizzly, grey mood I was trying to escape in the living room.

So my Trash Pad it was. Will couldn't hoover in there, since it had black bin bags for carpet (I'll explain that later too).

PLINK!!

The thumping music coming from the piano in the hall stopped dead the second I went to escape up the stairs.

"Tea won't be long!" Mum said in a strangely manic way, her hands frozen in a hover above the black and white keys.

Mum was mostly dreamy, not manic. Except when she was suffering overexposure to Nonna.

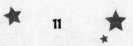

Had Nonna been particularly irritating to her since she came home from work today?

"Um, fine," I said with a shrug, wiggling my fingers at Martha, who was *boing, boing, boing*-ing in her bouncy chair at Mum's feet, keeping time with the music that had paused. "I'll just be in my room. Well, the spare room."

I corrected myself because Nonna was currently the tenant of *my* bedroom, and I was holed up in the Trash Pad. Which was a joy and not a torture, for sure. A girl can only take so much snoring and old lady potions and perfumes strewn around the place.

"Will's made something very special for tea!" said Mum, still with a manic glint in her eyes. "And Gran's coming!"

"Is that a good idea?" I asked Mum. Never mind boy-band wars; the Granny Wars had raged only a couple of weeks before.

Though I have to say that things had got a little better since Gran and Nonna had bonded over their shared excitement about Sonny's imminent superstar status, and Gran was carefully managing to overlap as little time as possible with Nonna.

But tea together? Was Mum crazy? Or had she turned into a bit of a gambler overnight and put a bet on with my dad about which of their

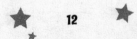

mothers was likely to start sniping at the other first?

"It'll be fine!" Mum insisted, pushing back a clump of dark, wavy hair that was escaping from the clips she had it pinned up with. "Will and I just thought it would be lovely to have a, um, lovely, special family meal together!"

Yeah ... we *really* needed a lovely, special family meal with two potentially feuding grannies on a Tuesday night. Big wow.

Just as I put a foot on the bottom stair, I felt myself being watched, and not just by Mum.

PHEN-yewwwwwwwwwww ... went the hoover, as Will flicked it off up on the top landing.

He smiled down at me, all nervous. As if he'd maybe hoovered up the cat by accident and wasn't looking forward to telling me.

"All right, Sadie?" he said, overly brightly, as I came up past him.

"Uh, yeah," I replied warily. Out of the corner of my eye, I could see Dog – our cat – padding out of the Trash Pad, now that the hoover racket had stopped. OK, so she wasn't inside the drum of the hoover, scrabbling to get out, then.

"Cool!" said Will, using his favourite-ever word a little too enthusiastically. "Did Mum tell you that we're all having a lovely—"

"—special family meal together," I finished for him. "Yep, she did."

BING-BONG!!

"That'll be Joan!" gasped Will, at the sound of the doorbell.

"I'll get it!!" yelped Mum, scurrying towards the door, even though Joan (otherwise known to me, Sonny and Martha as Gran) would have her key in the door any second, and would be calling out a cheerful "Yoo-hooo!" to whoever happened to be in.

Mum and Will – they were in what's commonly known as a tizz.

I had no idea what that was about, but I was obviously going to find out soon, if my grandmothers resisted bickering long enough to let anyone else get a word in edgeways during our "lovely, special family meal".

But for now, I'd go and chill in my yabbering-and tizz-free Trash Pad.

Last night, Sonny had given me a printed-out copy of a new publicity photo of his band.

I was sure I could pass a few happy minutes blacking out all the lads' teeth with a felt pen. . .

The Joy of the Trash Pad

"Miaow!" miaowed Dog.

I can't remember exactly how old I was when I'd insisted that our new pet kitty cat be called – confusingly – Dog. But I do remember that it was 'cause I just fancied being awkward at the time.

Dog – who'd seemed perfectly happy and unconfused by her name all these years – padded back into the Trash Pad, picking her paws up awkwardly as the bin-bag "carpet" rustled underfoot.

She was so busy watching her paws that she walked head first into Dad's old filing cabinet, which I was using as a very huge chest of drawers.

"Erpp!" she squawked.

"There you go!" I muttered, bending down to rub her furry forehead better. I wasn't too panicked. Dog hurting herself was pretty much the norm. For instance, on the day she got the all-clear from

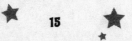

the vet over her torn cruciate ligament, Sonny managed to set her tail on fire (accidentally, honest). Dad once suggested that the vet should name a cage in the hospital room in her honour, since she was such a regular there.

"So, Dog . . . what do you think's going on with Mum and Will?" I muttered some more to her, now that I could see she was OK.

At the same time, I kicked off my Converse trainers (easy to do, since I always wear them with the heels folded down) and deposited Clyde on the squashy surface of the low-down, blow-up bed.

Dog purred, which was soothing – and proved she didn't have a catty concussion – but it wasn't really a very useful answer to my question.

So I picked up the marker pen and got ready to black out some teeth in the picture that I had taped to my wall, till I studied it and realized the band looked fine as they were, with the beards and spots I'd scribbled on them earlier.

Instead, I decided to press my computer into life and email Hannah and Letitia – my best buddies, who don't much like each *other*, sadly – some idle rubbish.

Moving the wooden picnic chair out from under the wrought-iron garden table (meet my

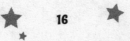

lookalike desk, etc.), I heard plastic rip. Ah, well, another hole in the "carpet", but that could easily be fixed with a bit of parcel tape, I thought, gazing at the zigzag pattern of wide, shiny brown tape across the floor.

I gazed some more at the rest of the room. It wasn't likely to be featured in any glam interiors magazines, that was for sure.

I mean, the fairy lights were nice, but the torn, peeling wallpaper wasn't. The clothes that weren't stashed in the filing cabinet were dangling in a tangle of mismatched hangers on the rail that Will had found in the street not so long ago (classy). My trainers were jumbled in a mini trainer hillock, alongside a teetering mountain of CDs and magazines. Actually, I think they'd all sort of merged together now that I was looking at it again. Not that it mattered. Unless I was particularly dozy one morning and tried to put the first Kings of Leon CD on my left foot instead of my trainer, I guess. . .

"It looks like one of those nuts art installations you get at Tate Modern," Hannah had said, grinning, last weekend when she, Letitia and me had finished our personalized drawings on a wall each.

We hadn't peeked at what we were doing while we were doing it. Oh no. We'd just squeaked away

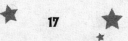

with our markers till we were all happy and finished, and then checked our handiwork out. On my wall, behind the bed, I'd drawn a grand, twirly headboard, with fat angels swooping overhead. On Letty's wall – the one with the window – there were now two extra windows drawn on either side, complete with flowerpots and a cross-eyed person waving in. Hannah had done her version of the skyline of London, though the dome of St Paul's Cathedral *did* look a bit like half an onion.

Being the kind, considerate sister I am (yeah, right!) I'd even let Sonny have a go on the last wall, by the door. But all he'd come up with was a squiggle that said "Sadie Rocks *rocks*!" on it (whoo, very imaginative!) and I'd since covered it up with a poster of The Drop Zone – the band I went to see with Dad, Will, Sonny and, of course, Cormac.

As for this room, well, once upon a time, the Trash Pad had been my old bedroom.

And here beginneth a short history lesson: in the days before I had taste, the walls were lemon yellow, with pink-painted shelves heaving with soft toys and Barbie dolls.

Then I got to about ten, and painted the walls a sort of mauve shade, and sold off all (well, *nearly*

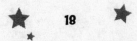

all) the Barbie dolls and soft toys and baby books at a table sale outside our house.

That was around the time that my mum and dad split up, though it was pretty hard for anyone on the outside to spot that fact, since my parents still got on all right-ish. The only difference was that Dad moved out of their bedroom and into his home office above the garage, where he turned into a forty-something-year-old teenager overnight, blaring music and surviving on delivery pizza.

It was only meant to be for a few weeks, till he got his own place, but three years later, Dad was *still* there, blaring out his old records and eating pepperoni pizza practically every night.

What *did* change in those three years was a) Mum meeting Will at the school where they both worked, b) Will moving in, c) baby Martha putting in an appearance and d) Dad's stomach getting ever bigger from his exclusively pizza-based diet.

Dad finally moved out a couple of months or so ago, to his new bachelor pad above the undertaker's (a real magnet for new girlfriends – not!).

Then back at home, there was a sudden game of musical rooms, with Sonny shifting into the office room above the garage, me switching to Sonny's vacated, much bigger bedroom, while *my* old room was left empty – ready to be transformed

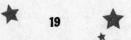

into a lemon yellow, soft-toy-infested den all over again, for *Martha* this time round.

Of course, the way things worked out, I had all of about two seconds(ish) to enjoy my new space, and then Nonna arrived, laden with endless suitcases, and instantly transformed my bedroom into a home-from-home for herself. Seeing what was going on, I was all set to camp out in my old room, till – sploosh!! – the water tank right above it went and burst, and the soggy plaster of the ceiling made its acquaintance with the carpet. . .

I tried bunking in with Nonna, but her road-drill snoring drove me nuts.

I tried bunking in with Sonny, which was (amazingly) all right for a while, till he started singing the deeply corny lyrics of his band's single in his sleep. ("*Oooooh, Momma, you always looked after me, and Dad, you're the man I wanna grow up to be, 'cause we are – yeah! Familyyyy!!*"). Bleurgh. . .

Then a week or so ago, the ceiling of my old room got replastered. And even though the carpet had been ripped out and the wallpaper was falling off the walls, it seemed like an oasis in the middle of my madhouse. So I moved in, Blu-tacking bin bags to the floor to solve the problem of splinters from bare floorboards interfacing with my bare feet.

My temporary hideout horrified Nonna. When she first saw it, she had tears in her eyes, and mumbled stuff about how she couldn't *bear* to think of her sweet granddaughter (that's *me*, by the way, in case you were confused by the description) living in a hovel like this.

But I was already getting kind of fond of my hovel.

It was going to be tough to move back into all the neatness next door once Nonna finally packed up and went. (Whenever that happy day would be. . .)

"Sadie, Mum says you've got to come downstairs now for tea," Sonny announced, suddenly bursting into my room without knocking. As usual.

"*SONNY!!*" I yelped at him.

"Oh, sorry, Sadie!" said Sonny, shuffling back outside and uselessly knocking. The big nerk.

"Come in. . ." I sighed. He came in. He grinned a slightly less full-on version of his usual chirpy grin, presumably still reeling from the shock of another teen boy band being on the scene.

"So are you coming?" he asked.

"Yeah, in a second," I muttered, looking around for my roll of parcel tape to fix the bin-bag carpet.

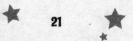

"Sonny, d'you know what Mum and Will are up to? What this whole 'lovely, special' family meal's about?"

"Nope," said Sonny, looking mildly surprised at the thought that it might be in any way unusual. That was *always* the way with Sonny; if something wasn't anything directly to do with him, he was oblivious to it.

"Just seems weird, that's all," I muttered, rifling hopefully for tape in a pile of random stuff.

"Hey!" exclaimed Sonny, as if a light bulb had pinged above his head. "Maybe they're going to announce they're getting married!"

I hadn't found the parcel tape, but I *had* found a clean sock not yet filed away in the drawer in the cabinet marked "KNICKERS & WHATEVER".

I balled up the sock and chucked it at Sonny's head.

"What?" He blinked, acting all stunned, as it unravelled and flopped limply on his shoulder.

"Well, *think* about it!" I sighed. "How can Mum and Will get married when Mum and Dad aren't even *divorced*? *Duh!*"

I knew I'd found myself calling Will my stepdad recently, but it was only because calling him my not-*quite*-stepdad took an awfully long time.

"Ahhhh. . ." murmured Sonny, my point

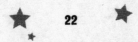

penetrating his thick skull.

Two minutes later, surrounded by grannies and a table heaving with particularly great food, Sonny was "ahhing" again.

"Ahhh!!!!!!"

The multiple exclamation marks after this particular "ahhh" were because (cue my shocked expression) Mum and Will had just announced they were getting *married*. . .

"Oh, Nicola!" gasped Gran, all teary-eyed, jumping up from her seat to hug Mum and then Will.

Little Martha – getting jiggled in Gran's arms – started slapping her chubby fingers together and giggling, though she hadn't a clue what was happening.

"Darling! How lovely!!" shrieked Nonna, clasping her hands together. She was probably planning her mother-of-the-bride outfit already. "Oh, I *do* love weddings!"

"Yes, we know," I heard Gran mutter under her breath.

Nonna liked getting married so much she'd done it three times. The first time to my granddad Bernard, who'd died before me and Sonny were born; the second to Alejandro, a restaurant owner in Spain (a marriage which lasted about as long as a summer holiday); and lastly to Jack, a fellow retired Brit settled in Nonna's adopted hometown of Mojacar, who died when I was little, of either extreme old age or as a cunning way of avoiding listening to Nonna's endless wittering – I'm not entirely sure which.

"So when's the big day?" asked Nonna, oblivious to Gran's mumbled aside.

"Well, that's the amazing thing – it's happening in less than two weeks' time!" Mum smiled, all fluttery and flappy with happiness.

"What?!" both grans squeaked in tandem.

"I know!" laughed Mum. "Will and I had been talking about getting married recently, but we hadn't planned on it happening so soon. It was just that Will went to Islington Town Hall last week to look into possible dates, and found out there'd been a short notice cancellation."

"I booked it straight away, but we didn't want to make it definite and tell you all till I checked with my dad that he could come," Will joined in, stretching a hand across the table to hold Mum's. (His fingers tidied away a couple of crumbs on the way. A bit of romance didn't get in the way of his obsessive-compulsive tendencies, I noticed.)

"Ted just got back to Will today to say he's

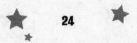

24

managed to get someone to look after his farm, so . . . well, it's all systems go!" Mum said brightly. "And of course, I thought since *you'd* still be here, Mum, it would be perfect, really!"

"Oh, Nicola, darling! That is the *sweetest* thing!!" Nonna said, holding her hands to her chest and looking genuinely moved.

Ahem. Hold it with the party atmosphere, I thought to myself. Weren't they all ignoring a teeny, tiny HUMUNGOUS problem?!

"Mum. . ." I said, aware that I was the only one not about to faint with the excitement of the whole spontaneous wedding announcement. "Aren't you and Dad still technically *married*?!"

Everyone turned to look at me, as if I was a real party-pooper, I swear. Well, *excuse* me for being boringly practical.

"Well, that's the brilliant thing!" Mum said, brightening up again. "Your dad and I did all the paperwork *ages* ago and sort of forgot about it. But I checked with the solicitor and it turns out the divorce becomes final next week, so it all fits together really nicely!"

Hmm. How "brilliant" and "really nice", indeed.

"Ooh, isn't that wonderful, darling?" Nonna crooned some more. "Though it must be strange for *you*, Joan, dear. . ."

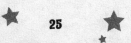

Nonna had turned to Gran, who had been happily bouncing Martha on her knee till she saw Nonna tilt her head to the side and throw her a condescending look.

Uh-oh.

Nonna had several personalities (funny, kind, tactless and mad for starters), and the tactless one was just about to surface again, I was sure.

"Why is that, *Muriel?*" asked Gran, warily.

Nonna winced. She hated being called "Muriel" as much as she hated being called "Granny". She endlessly tried to get everyone to call her Bunny – the nickname her friends in Spain called her – but Gran wasn't having any of it.

"Well, because once my Nicola is officially divorced from your Martin—"

"*Max,*" said Mum and Gran at the same time.

Nonna swept away their correction as if it was as irrelevant as a fly at a rubbish dump. "I just mean that once Nicola and *Max* are divorced, you won't be part of the family any more, will you?"

"Of course she will!" Mum practically yelped, a giant smile plastered on her face, as she tried not to show how embarrassed she was by her own mother's tact-free comments. "Joan will *always* be part of the family!!"

"Hey, maybe my band could play at the wedding

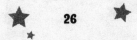

reception!" Sonny jumped in, saving the day with his suggestion. "Our single's called 'We Are Family', remember!"

As everyone let themselves be sidetracked (to avoid an escalation of the Granny Wars), I sat back and thought of someone who wasn't here.

A someone who might not think the current happy, clappy news was either "amazing", "brilliant" or even just "really nice".

And that someone was called *Dad*. . .

Romeo and, er, Nicola...

Dad and Mum, Mum and Dad...

They were like Romeo and Juliet: a mad, crazy love that was destined never to be. (Well, if you replaced the teenage, tragic Juliet with Nicola, an airhead music teacher, and handsome young Romeo with Max, a middle-aged paper-plate wholesaler.)

The thing was, when they split up, Mum moved on – to Will, to be precise. And let's face it, Dad didn't move on at *all*. He didn't even move out of the *house* till it was getting to be an embarrassment.

Which seemed to me, if I pretended to be a smart psychologist-type person, to mean he hadn't had "closure".

Oh, yep, I was pretty sure that underneath his collection of loud Hawaiian shirts, Dad's heart still beat for his one true love: his own airhead, classical-music-obsessed version of Juliet...

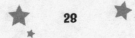

"I can't believe this!" said Dad, shaking his head.

I bit the rag-nail on my finger and gazed at him, standing in his first-floor living room above the undertaker's, hovering by his stereo, staring into space.

I'd worried all last night in bed about telling him The News.

I'd worried all day at school, getting Letitia nearly as stressed out as I was with the, er, stress of it all.

I'd worried *after* school, sitting under our pet Christmas tree. I got all maudlin too, remembering how Dad had planted it here in the copse behind the house when Sonny and me were just two, and had been in floods of tears at the idea of our branch-covered buddy being chucked out with the post-festive trash.

Huddled under the Christmas tree late this afternoon, I got to thinking about the years Dad had tried to educate me and Sonny in the history of popular music (well, *his* version) by playing us endless ancient albums and not-so-ancient CDs in his hideout above the garage.

I remembered too all the fun (well, as much fun as you can have with Sonny in the room) we'd had watching movies and comedy DVDs together, with a stash of pizza (of course) and vats of ice cream to keep us company.

Ah, my sweet, thoughtful, kind dad.

Wow, I loved him.

Um, *mostly*.

I mean, I really *didn't* love the way his very loud Hawaiian shirt was missing a button and his round, slightly fuzz-covered belly was currently peeking out. And I really wished he'd stop it with the sandy-brown Elvis quiff and sideburns look he'd been rocking recently.

Still, poor Dad. . .

I stared at him now, as he carried on with the head-shaking, his quiff wobbling with the effort.

Me and Sonny came here for tea most Wednesdays, and most Wednesdays, I really looked forward to it. But not today, 'cause of The News I had to break to him, since everyone else was too giddy with imminent wedding fever to spare him a thought.

"Sadie, you're honestly telling me –" he stopped and rubbed his face, aghast – "that I've *never* let you hear one of the *best* sixties records ever?!"

"Nope," I said, wishing Dad would shut up about music for one minute and let me say what I had to say.

"Well, wrap your ears around this – 'The Tracks

Of My Tears', by Smokey Robinson. Unrequited love never sounded so good!"

Urgh . . . not only did Dad sound like the corniest DJ in the universe there, but he'd just rediscovered a song that couldn't be more appropriate. Unless, of course, there was a song around called "Nicola, I Wish We'd Never Split Up".

As soon as the *"Doo-doo-doo-doo, doo-do-doo-doo!"* backing vocals began, Dad closed his eyes and started swaying. It wasn't the ideal time to go blabbing The News, but let's face it, *no* time was going to be a *good* time. . .

"Dad, I've—"

CLATTER, CLATTER, CLATTER, THUNKETTY, CLATTER, THUNK!!!

That wasn't the chorus of "The Tracks Of My Tears". That was Sonny and Cormac bouncing down the metal staircase outside the living-room window, coming from the flat above. They bounded into Dad's flat like a couple of overenthusiastic dogs, through the glass-panelled fire-escape door.

Nice timing, lads.

"Check it out!" yelped Sonny, tapping the bowler hat on his head. "Kyle lent it to me!"

"Well, Kyle doesn't *know* I've lent it to you yet – but I'm sure he'll be fine about it," Cormac chipped in.

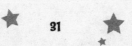

31

Cormac McConnell. How do I explain him? Well, he was Dad's upstairs neighbour, along with his big brother, Kyle, and he worked in McConnell & Sons Funeral Directors, which was downstairs from Dad's flat. Yep, he was your average, normal, seventeen-year-old trainee undertaker who had a sideline in stand-up comedy. He was also my friend Letty's Fantasy Boyfriend (not that Cormac had any idea about that).

Anyway, I'd seen that bowler hat before. It had been hanging off an antler, which in turn belonged to a fake stag's head (*please* let it have been a fake head) upstairs in the boys' flat. It was amazing I'd even remembered seeing it, since Kyle's hobby of furnishing the place with strange theatrical props and kitsch second-hand stuff meant your eyeballs sort of melted when you tried to take it all in.

"So?" I said with a shrug, watching as Sonny began doing a dance routine to "Tracks Of My Tears", tipping the hat off his head and holding it over his heart. "What's the point?"

"Part of a new stage costume, Sonny?" Dad asked with an amused smile, turning the volume down.

"Exactly!" Sonny replied, plopping it back on his head at a rakish angle. "We've got to film our

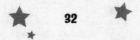

video on Saturday, and we need a new look. We can't dress in T-shirts and baseball caps if The Twist are wearing that same sort of stuff!"

Thank goodness. I'd witnessed the awfulness of the baseball caps, fitted T-shirts and neon cycling shorts (*bleurgh!*) at close quarters, and it wasn't a pretty sight. Especially the time Kennedy did a kung-fu-style jump at rehearsals with dire consequences, thanks to a pair of overly tight shorts and a weak seam. (Yuck – I might need several sessions of therapy to forget that flash of Spider-Man pants. . .)

"You mean, you're all going to be wearing *those*?!" I asked, wondering where Kennedy was going to find a bowler hat big enough to fit on his bowl-sized head.

"Maybe," said Sonny, shrugging. "It's just something to suggest to Benny tomorrow. Him and Angie have got a meeting with the video director tomorrow afternoon."

OK, Benny I knew. He was the lecturer from the stage school who a) looked like he wanted to burst into song at any minute, as if he was living his life like it was an Andrew Lloyd Webber musical, and b) had put the band together and was now managing it.

"Who's Angie?" I asked, racking my brain.

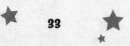

Dad suddenly burst out coughing.

"She's the publicity girl from the record company," Sonny reminded me, as he helpfully thumped Dad on the back.

Oh, yeah. At the party the record company threw – when the lads had signed their contracts – Angie had been stuck with Dad, listening to him listing his favourite all-time records in alphabetical order while she smiled bravely and looked over his shoulder for someone more interesting to talk to.

"Oooh, what's going on in here?" came a down-to-earth Irish voice, as my gran bustled into the room and headed straight for the kitchenette with a carrier bag full of vegetable-shaped knobbles in it.

By the way, what was it with my grannies? *Neither* of them seemed to be planning on moving back to their actual homes any time soon. It wasn't just Nonna and her Spanish apartment; it was also Gran and her bungalow in Barnet. She was currently staying in Dad's spare room (spare *cupboard* more like), to "help him settle in", and had made herself indispensable, cooking meals with actual *vitamins* in them, and adding a few homely touches, such as ornaments on top of the boy-toy speakers and sleek black gadgets and gizmos Dad that had filled the living room with.

(Yeah – as if living above an undertaker's wasn't bad enough, try luring potential new girlfriends to a bachelor pad with a resident sixty-something-year-old *mother* in it. But there you go – psychologically speaking, maybe Dad *didn't* want to attract any girlfriends, since he was still pining for Mum. . .?!)

"Hi, Gran!" Sonny greeted her cheerfully, like the human golden retriever that he was. "Well, since you ask, *Dad's* having a coughing fit, *Cormac's* maybe come up with a new look for the band for the video we're doing on Saturday, and *Sadie* . . . Sadie's just scowling."

I hadn't thought I was scowling before, but I sure was *now*. Anyway, how could Sonny be so cheery after yesterday's wedding announcement and how it might affect Dad? Well, because his mind was so vacuous and self-absorbed that he'd never think that there might possibly be a chance that Dad would take the news badly.

Help; I *really* needed to tell Dad. I'd asked yesterday at our "lovely, special family meal" if *I* could be the one to break it to Dad, and this was my chance. I couldn't go home tonight without spilling the beans. He couldn't go on being the last to know. But with Gran and Sonny and Cormac swarming about with vegetables and stupid hats, how was I going to get the chance?

"Come with me," I ordered my still-spluttering dad. "You need a drink of water."

Grabbing him by the elbow, I led him out of the living room and into the bathroom, off the small square hall.

Phew: it had an overpowering, chemical, floral smell about it – which was coming from a bowl of luminous yellow pot pourri placed on top of the cistern (a Gran purchase, for sure). And Dad had been doing some home improvements in here, I noticed. There was a giant framed poster of Oasis above the toilet.

"Here," I said, making him sit down on the loo, right under Liam Gallagher, and sip water from a flowery plastic tumbler (*another* Gran purchase, I bet).

As he drank, I took a deep breath, knowing *now* was the time. . .

"Ah, that's better!" Dad said first, as his coughing fit eased off. "Hey, can you believe our Sonny's going to be doing a video? I can't wait to see it on the telly! Wonder what it'll get shown on? One of the music channels, I suppose. . ."

Who was Dad kidding? A bunch of thirteen-

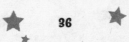

year-old boys crooning about how much they loved their mummies? The only channel that would show stuff like that would be The Saddo Channel, and as that hadn't been invented yet, it didn't seem like there'd be much of a chance of seeing Sonny and Co. dancing around in their bowler hats or chicken costumes or whatever they decided was their new image.

"We'll never be able to watch it at home anyway," I muttered instead, taking the empty tumbler back from Dad. "Not on that midget TV we've got at the moment."

"No!" gasped Dad. "Tell me you're not *still* using that! What about the big telly? All it needed was a new cable!"

Clyde was to blame. He'd nibbled through the TV cable, in case it tasted of lettuce or something equally delicious. It was just lucky that he hadn't turned himself into hot, toasted bunny. . .

Will had ordered a new cable from the tiny TV repair shop nearby, and while we waited (and waited) for the replacement to come, we'd all been huddled round Mum's ancient portable with binoculars.

"Well, the shop's still not had the right cable delivered," I told Dad, itching to tell him something else entirely.

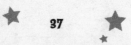

"But you can get a cable like that at *any* big electrical shop!" gasped Dad, slapping his hands on his thighs.

"Really? What – you mean we've spent weeks with eye strain when there was no need?" I asked.

"Too right!" Dad laughed. "Look, I'll pick one up myself when I'm out on a delivery this week, and set it up for you. Huh! What's Will like? Didn't realize your mum was marrying someone so useless!"

Um . . . *what* did Dad just say there?

"You – you *know*?!" I mumbled, stunned.

"Yeah, your gran said when she got in last night," said Dad, still smiling. "She was in a right state, thinking I'd be all upset ab—"

The ringtone of the Red Hot Chili Peppers' "Give It Away" trilled from the top pocket of Dad's shirt.

"'Scuse a second, Sadie, honey," said Dad, checking the caller ID and going slightly pink. I think he was hoping I might leave, but my legs in particular seemed too stunned to move anywhere.

"HEY, HOW'RE YOU DOING!" Dad boomed, as if he was talking to a particularly deaf person with a poor signal on the moon. "YEAH – I'M

STILL GOOD FOR TONIGHT. NINE. . .? YEAH."

He was talking to Kemal or Daryl, I was sure. They worked together all day, sang along to the radio together all day, and if that wasn't enough, spent several evenings a week watching football matches together in the pub.

"I'M HAVING SOME TIME WITH MY KIDS JUST NOW, BUT I'LL SEE YOU THERE. LOOKING FORWARD TO IT, ANGIE!"

Angie?

My dad was going out later to meet someone called Angie?! Was this a *date*?! And if that wasn't weird enough, this person my dad might be going out on a date with had the same name as the young, trendy, bored-looking record company girl that Sonny had just been talking about. What were that chances of *that* happening?

"Angie," said Dad sheepishly, slipping the phone back in his pocket. "From the record company. Got her number at that party a while back, but never got round to calling her. Till today. Hearing your mum's news sort of inspired me to get on with it, y'know?"

Er, no, I'm not sure I *did* know.

All I knew was that I was standing in a bathroom that smelled of chemical flowers, with a man who

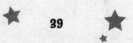

looked like an Elvis impersonator with bad taste in shirts, being stared at menacingly by Liam Gallagher.

I was sure I didn't remember a scene like this in *Romeo and Juliet*. . .

My brother, the nerk

There were lots of things I wished were different.

I was lying on my blow-up bed – under the watchful eye of my marker-pen angels – and writing a list of them now. Directly on to the wall.

I'd started doing it because my head was kind of buzzing, and I was trying really, really hard to distract myself from the thought of Dad grooving away embarrassingly to some band in the Dublin Castle bar in Camden with a girl called Angie. . .

And so here was my list, which was written in gold gel pen (only the best for my peeling wood-chip wallpaper).

1. I wish Clyde would stop chewing holes in my favourite stuff.

(I'd just spotted a hole in the toe of my Converse trainers, and in the middle of a magazine I hadn't started reading yet.)

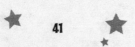

2. I wish Dog would stop falling off things or getting hurt or generally sick for a while.

(She was sitting sneezing at the bottom of my bed, making it jiggle. Cat flu and expensive vet's bills ahoy.)

3. I wish Nonna would stop pretending to know everything when she clearly doesn't.

(When me and Sonny came in from Dad's, I heard her telling a tense-looking Will that goldfish were nocturnal.)

4. I wish Nonna would stop making us watch repeats of A Place In The Sun.

(She was addicted to shows about people moving abroad. I just wished her builders would finally finish her flat so *she* could move abroad, where it would be easier to love her from a distance.)

5. I wish Letitia and Hannah would start liking each other, so I could moan to them about my life while they were in the same room, instead of having to repeat myself.

(I'd just been wittering away to each of them in turn on my mobile, using up twice as much credit. Boo.)

6. I wish Dad wasn't on a date with a girl who is much younger than him.

(Though Will was ten years younger than Mum,

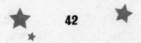

so maybe I should get used to this family tradition.)

7. *I wish me and Sonny were the sort of twins who were psychic.*

(Then I could figure out what exactly was filling his head, 'cause it sure wasn't brains. On the way home, I tried to explain my theory of Dad dating on the rebound, and he just didn't get it.)

8. *I wish I wasn't starting to worry about what I was going to have to wear to Mum and Will's wedding.*

(Mum had informed me when we got in from Dad's that me, her and both my grans were going on a wedding outfit shopping hunt on Saturday afternoon. Sigh. I'd rather do work experience at a funeral with Cormac, if I had the choice. . .)

"Hey, Sadie!" said Sonny, barging into my room without knocking AGAIN!

"Sonny! Would you please not DO that!!" I yelled at him, grabbing a pillow to cover my scribbles and leaning back on it. "I could've been. . ."

I dreaded to think of all the things I could've been doing. I just knew I didn't want anyone seeing me doing whatever that was.

Maybe I should have torn off a long strip of

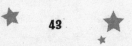

wallpaper – a strip big enough to pin to the whole of the front of the door to this room – and spray-painted "KNOCK FIRST, YOU BIG NERK!!" on it. I'd definitely do it, if I didn't think Mum would get all upset. She'd just love it if Sonny and me were all cutesy inseparable, but that was as likely to happen as Mum giving up classical piano and taking up MC-ing at hip-hop clubs.

"Yeah, yeah . . . knock, knock, knock," said Sonny wearily, miming a knock or three. "Sadie, you've *got* to see something. . ."

And with that, he strode over to my computer and hit the space bar to bring it to life.

He called up the Google search page so fast, he didn't seem to notice that my screensaver said "SONNY BIRD IS A NERK!" on it, OR the graffiti'd photo of his band Blu-tacked to the wall behind.

In that case, he'd never notice the wish list I'd been scribbling on the wall. I chucked the pillow away (accidentally hitting Dog on the head, of course) and got myself up to see what exactly was getting my brother all agitated.

"Check it out!" Sonny almost hissed.

Ooh. On screen were five teenage boys in baseball caps, T-shirts and skater shorts, standing at the top of one of those old-fashioned helter-

44

skelter fairground rides. As the opening bars of some dreamy-sounding music played, each boy in turn slid down, and was freeze-framed at the bottom with their name flashed up under them: "D'wayne"; "Benjii"; "Jax"; "Harley"; "Tiger".

Urgh . . . The Twits' names were worse than *Sonny's* band's.

Uh-oh . . . but their song was better. By that, I mean it was still *rubbish*, only it was a better standard of rubbish than Sadie Rocks' first, awful single.

"Just wanna hold your hand, girl! It would mean everything to meeeeeee," crooned Benjii, wandering past a hook-a-duck stall, his big puppy-dog eyes gazing directly into the camera lens.

In the background, the other four lads trailed behind him, holding cuddly toys they were supposed to have won at the hit-a-can stall or something, and harmonized with *"Ooooh, say you will, girl, say you will, girl!"*

"What do you think?" Sonny asked me.

I know I got a kick out of winding Sonny up a lot of the time, but I didn't want to come over all Nonna-ish and say something tactless. So I tried turning the question around.

"Yeah, but what do *you* think?" I asked him right back.

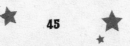

45

"I think they're really good. Which is *bad*," he muttered.

It was then that I noticed he was wearing a stripy T-shirt that looked very familiar. Mainly because it was mine.

"What's with this?" I demanded, yanking at the hem of my top, which I'd last seen in the laundry basket.

"Just playing around with different new looks," said Sonny, still gawping at The Twits, like the big twit he was. "Thought it might go well with the bowler hat. . ."

ARGHHH!! That's the thing with Sonny. There I was, feeling a tiny bit sorry for him and trying to restrain myself from telling him the cold, hard truth, and he was just thinking of himself, as usual.

"Ooh, you're *so* selfish!" I barked at him, physically manhandling my T-shirt off his back.

"What?" I heard Sonny giggle, from somewhere inside all the material. "Just 'cause I borrowed your T-shirt?"

ARGHHH *again*! Being laughed at when you're mad just makes you MADDER!!

I *had* to get him back. It would be too easy for him to make a joke of me huffing over my unlawfully borrowed H&M top. I had to think of *something* that might make him stop and think.

And then I remembered what Cormac had said to me one day last week.

"It's not *just* about my T-shirt. It's about your whole *attitude*! What about Cormac, hmm?"

"What *about* Cormac?" said Sonny, emerging from my T-shirt with a bare chest, rumpled hair and a confused expression.

"A few weeks ago, you promised to introduce him to that comedian guy."

Sonny still looked confused.

"He used to be a student at your stage school? You said he came to do a talk there? He's just won awards and is going out on his first big comedy tour?" I tried to prompt my brain-dead brother. "You said you'd arrange for Cormac to meet him sometime!"

Sonny seemed to have forgotten already, even though Cormac hadn't. ("Has Sonny mentioned anything about Martin Shore?" he'd asked me shyly, when I'd met him on the stairs going up to Dad's flat.)

"Oh, yeah! Martin Shore!" muttered Sonny, his mind slowly creaking into life.

"Yes, him! And do you know how much that meant to Cormac? The idea of talking to a *real* stand-up comedian, when that's his *dream* job?"

My dopey brother blinked, lost in thought.

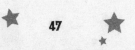

At last. Sonny looked like it had *finally* sunk in that other people's feelings mattered.

He opened his mouth to say something. Maybe he was about to tell me that he was off to phone Cormac, or maybe even to apologize to me for nicking my top.

"Hey, Sadie, you know the video shoot we're doing on Saturday?"

ARGHHH yet *again*!! I buried my head in my T-shirt and shook it.

There was *no* getting through to Sonny, or getting him off his favourite subject – i.e., *Sonny*.

"I just remembered," he burbled on, ignoring the fact that I had my head in my hands (and T-shirt), "Benny texted me to say that the director thinks it would be really cool if you were in it. The video, I mean. Since you're Sadie and everything."

My heart stood still and my eyes went wide – though I couldn't see anything except very close-up stripes and a label that read "100% cotton".

It wasn't so much an "ARGHHH" moment as a full-on "*EEEEEKKKKK!!!*"...

Every size of black cloud. . .

"Awwwwww! Sadie, look!!"

"What is it?" I asked, squinting at the furry, fluffy thing Letitia had picked up off the toy-shop shelf.

Letitia was a bit of a fluffy thing herself – well, fluffy-headed at least. Her hobbies were cooing at cute things, doing gymnastics, and falling temporarily in love with people who had no idea she was in love with them. (Like I said before, Cormac was her current Fantasy Boyfriend. Though next week, it was just as likely to be some random boy in the background of *High School Musical 3*, or a smiley lad in a washing-powder ad in one of her mum's magazines. She wasn't fussy.)

Anyway, I didn't know whether the furry, fluffy thing she was holding was meant to be a bush baby or an owl, but I reckoned it could make a pretty funny-but-funky birthday present for Letty's soon-to-be-six-years-old little sis.

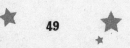

In fact, once I moved out of the Trash Pad and it got transformed into a frilly Martha Pad, it would be kind of nice to come in here and get *my* kid sis some furry, fluffy room-warming presents.

"I think it's a little hot-water-bottle cover, maybe," Letitia answered my question with a frown, as she ferreted about at the back of all the fur for buttons or Velcro or other clues.

"Do you think so?" I said dubiously, hoping she wasn't about to tear a seam and get charged for breakages.

"Whatever . . . isn't this the *cutest*? Oh. . ."

That was the quickest flip-around from enthusiasm to flatness I'd ever heard.

I looked at the cute-mutant-bush-baby-owl-thing for signs of something-going-wrong-ness, but that didn't seem to have caused the "Oh. . ."

Then I followed Letty's gaze, and saw who'd just come in the door of the shop.

"Hi!" said Hannah, hoicking her heavy school bag up on to her shoulder as she gave me – and Letty too, hopefully – a wave. (By the way, Hannah's hobbies were: acting cool; wearing famous rock band logo T-shirts, even though she'd never listened to any music by those bands; and working out ways she could get rid of her hideous younger brother, Harry.)

So *Hannah* was the reason for Letty's "Oh. . ." Hmm. *Great* to see how totally joyful my best friend number one (Letty) was to see my best friend number two (Hannah), and vice versa. Every time I thought they were starting to get along better, *blam!*, they slipped right back into acting super-uninterested in each other. It was *so* boring.

At least I'd realized a long time ago that it was a good job Hannah didn't go to the same school as me and Letty, or I'd get an ulcer from the stress of them acting all "whatever!" around each other the entire day, *every* single day.

"Just spotted you guys through the window when I was passing," Hannah continued, glancing around at the gingham squashy fluffiness of the shop. "Wow, I'd have wanted to come and *live* in this place when I was younger!"

The inside of Frogs and Fairies was just about as opposite from my Trash Pad as it was possible to get. It was a pastel, gorgeous kiddie heaven, compared to the parcel-taped, graffiti'd scuzz-space I was currently living in.

"Letty's looking for something for her sister Charonna's birthday," I explained, so Hannah wouldn't think I was trying to accessorize the Trash Pad with a china dolly tea set or a nursery characters revolving night light.

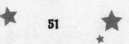

"Yeah?" said Hannah, glancing uninterestedly (what else?) at the cute-mutant-bush-baby-owl-thing. "Anyway, I'm glad I saw you, Sadie, 'cause I was going to ask you something. . ."

"What? Why I'm so effortlessly *stylish* all the time?" I jokily guessed, striking a pose, specially to show off my school trousers and the trainers with the hole bitten out of the toe by Clyde.

"No." Hannah grinned, though she was looking a bit sheepish.

Normally, if Hannah was looking a bit sheepish, it was because she wanted me to do something truly awful, like help her babysit her brother, Harry.

If she was about to try and emotionally blackmail me into *that*, I'd have to refuse. I'd rather be forced to listen to Sonny's rotten single on a loop for forty-eight hours *straight* than go through the torture of being a sitting target for one of Harry's endless practical jokes again. A girl can only stand being hurt and humiliated by a weaselly ten-year-old so many times. I still sometimes suffered panic attacks about going for a wee, half-expecting to find cling film stretched across the loo. . .

"Can I come along to the video shoot, *please*?! Pretty please with sprinkles on top?" Hannah pleaded, holding her hands together in front of her and then dropping to her knees in full-on begging mode. "I won't get in the way, I promise! I just really want to watch!!"

The video shoot. It was happening tomorrow morning at 7 a.m., on Holloway Road, this really big main road near where we live. It's kind of long, busy and slightly grotty. The director had picked it because of its "urban quality", Sonny had explained (yeah, and "urban quality" is just a posh way of saying "slightly grotty").

All I could think of was all the drivers going by, laughing at Sonny and the other lads doing some dumb dance routine along the pavement. With me popping up like a lemon in the middle of it all. . .

Why had I said yes?

Oh, yeah: 'cause of sheer stubbornness. 'Cause Nonna had happened to pass the door when Sonny was asking me, and said, "But, Sonny, darling, Sadie isn't an actress!", which of course made me determined to do it, just to show her.

How useless was that? Of course, *now* I'd realized I'd made a huge mistake. And it wasn't the sort of thing where I could ask my mum to write a sick note to get me out of it. . .

"Sadie already said that *I* could go!" said Letty with a smile, chuffed that she had one over on Hannah.

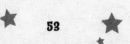

"So I can come too? Please?" Hannah asked hopefully, scrabbling up to her feet again.

"Yeah, whatever," I said casually, though really I was relieved to think I'd have two allies on the sidelines. If the director asked me to do something *completely* mortifying, I could maybe arrange for them to pelt him with eggs or something.

"Yay!" squealed Hannah. "This is so exciting! And then there's the wedding next Saturday too!"

Mum and Will were having a teeny-weeny wedding ceremony starring the two of them, with me and Martha as bridesmaids, Sonny as Will's best man, plus just three guests (Nonna, Gran and Will's dad, Ted, coming up from his farm in Cornwall).

But then there was going to be a party back at the house, with gallons of friends and an overload of catering, since Gran would go into a cooking and baking frenzy for sure.

It was tough – when it came to the wedding, I wanted to be as excited as Hannah and Letty, but every time I started to get all sunshiny about it, a couple of black clouds of gloom kept getting in the way... The smaller cloud was the stupid shopping trip I was going to have to go on with Mum, Nonna and Gran tomorrow afternoon (granny-frock shopping – what could be more grim than that? Probably the "nice frocks" they'd want to see *me* in). The *bigger* cloud was Dad-shaped. What was he thinking? How was he feeling? I hadn't seen him since Wednesday. How had his (urgh) "date" gone?

"Y'know, I think I'm going to get this," I heard Letty say, and found myself trailing after her as she walked over to the counter with the cute-mutant-bush-baby-owl-thing. Hannah trailed too, dragging her bag along the floor.

"So what time do we have to be there tomo—" Hannah began to say, until she – along with me and Letty – suddenly spotted the shocked and startled expression on the face of the shop assistant manning the till. The woman was staring out of the big glass window, at something *truly* bad, you could tell. Had she just seen a crash? An ex-boyfriend kissing a new girlfriend? A spaceship landing in the middle of the road?

Nope.

It was even *more* terrible than all of that.

It was a bum.

A bum mooning up against the glass.

A bum attached to a ten-year-old boy, who was a weasel in disguise.

"HARRY!" yelped Hannah, stomping at high

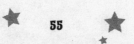

speed towards the door, looking like she was going to whack her heavy school bag round her brother's head when she got outside. "I *TOLD* him to wait out there and not get into any trouble!!"

Expecting Harry not to get into any trouble was like hoping scientists would announce new findings that proved crisps and chocolate were vital to a balanced diet. It was *never* going to happen.

Then – as if she was waking out of her daytime nightmare – the shop assistant turned and stared at Letty and me. You could sense that she thought we were somehow connected to the weasel currently defacing her window. (She'd be getting the dusters and spray cleaner out the second we'd disappeared.)

Letty panicked first, dropping the cute-mutant-bush-baby-owl-thing into a nearby basket and fleeing.

The panic was infectious, and I did some fleeing of my own, knowing in an instant that I'd never be able to shop for Martha-friendly lovely things in here ever again. . .

Never mind clouds of gloom; living with Harry must have been like trying to survive in the middle of a cyclone of *dread*.

"Do you think it would be against the law for

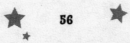

Hannah to fix a padlock on his door when he was asleep?" Letty had asked, with touching sympathy, when we last saw Hannah, storming off towards her house, yelling into her mobile, letting her mum know *exactly* what Harry had been up to this time. The Weasel had been trailing behind her, casually flicking elastic bands at the ankles of passers-by.

"She'd be better off trying to sell him to a zoo," I'd suggested instead, heading for my own house. "Maybe she could swap him with something cuddlier, like a viper, or a stingray. . ."

As I'd joked, I felt the gloom of my own personal clouds settle over me. There was nothing much I could do about the shopping trip, *or* the video shoot hell I'd signed up for, but maybe I'd be able to shoo away the cloud with Dad's name on it. I needed to see him, to see how he was doing.

So instead of heading home, I took a diversion and found myself on the street where his work unit was. I could see it in the distance, the big metal shutters rolled up, masses of stacked cardboard boxes inside.

And as I got closer, I spotted Dad – uh-oh – with his head in his hands! With his head in his hands, and Kemal and Daryl looking at him worriedly. . .

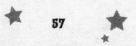

This was not good. At *all*.

I sped up, practically breaking into a run (not easy to do in slip-on trainers), and hurried towards him.

"*YESSS!!*" Dad suddenly exploded, as I got within a couple of metres of him.

He was grinning and punching the air. Kemal and Daryl broke into spontaneous applause.

"Dad?" I said, slowing down, completely confused.

"Hey, Sadie!" he replied, spinning around at the sound of my voice. "1975! I got it!"

"Got what?" I asked. What did he get in 1975? His first car? A terrible disease?

Dad pointed at the radio. Aha . . . he was addicted to music quizzes on some station he always had it tuned in to. I should have known. . .

"1975 – the year 10cc had a hit with 'I'm Not In Love'!" He beamed at me.

He high-fived Kemal and Daryl as he spoke, and held his hand out for one from me. I limply slapped the hand of the King of Pop Trivia. . .

"So what brings you down to my thriving business empire, Sadie baby?" Dad joked. "Can't bear not to see your dear old daddy?"

"Something like that," I replied, as casually as I could.

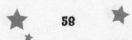

I want to know how your date went, I thought, wondering how to subtly broach the subject.

"Guess you want to know how my date went!" he said brightly, as I felt my cheeks pink up in surprise.

"Whatever," I said with a shrug.

"Well, it was pretty . . . excellent, actually!"

Hmm – from the grin and the body language, Dad looked kind of pleased with himself. Maybe he *wasn't* pining for Mum. Maybe my instincts were *wrong*.

"I mean, Angie's great! Though mostly we spoke about Sonny and the lads, and the single coming up next week, and the video, of course. Oh!"

Just like Letty earlier, a shadow seemed to suddenly pass over Dad's face with that "Oh!"

"Seeing you has just reminded me – I said I'd get that TV cable for your mum, didn't I?" he mumbled, looking deep in thought. "Tell her I'll be round soon, will you?"

Hmm. Maybe my instincts were right after *all*. . .

Weird, in the circumstances

"Sadie! Sadie! Sadie!" a small girl shouted, waving at me as if I was a member of Girls Aloud or something.

"Shush! Leave her alone! She's doing an important job!" I heard Letitia say to her kid sister, Charonna.

Ha! A very important job? I didn't *think* so. Here's what was going on. . .

The time: 7.50 a.m., Saturday morning.

The setting: Holloway Road, just outside the office shop. It had opened up early specially, with its regular, weird forest of whirly-wheeled, different-coloured office chairs displayed outside on the pavement. ("Great background colour!" according to Richie, the video director.)

The characters: five enthusiastic boy-band members in various mismatching bizarre outfits, and a very embarrassed girl called Sadie, who'd been forced to wear a bright red T-shirt with the "Sadie Rocks" logo on it. Oh, *dear*. . .

"I can't do this," I muttered to Cormac's brother, Kyle, as he dotted a soft, powdery brush over my face, while we stood in the make-up area for the video shoot (i.e., in the doorway of a shabby, locked-up pub).

Thank goodness for Kyle. I'd met him a few times before at his mad flat upstairs from Dad's, and knew he a) was part of the McConnell dynasty of undertakers, b) was a make-up artist for ads and fashion shows and music videos and other impressive stuff, and c) had learnt his craft from doing fabulous makeovers on dead people so that grieving relatives gasped at their drop-dead (ahem) gorgeousness.

I just hadn't known that Sonny had suggested Kyle for this shoot. ("I'm just here to check my props don't get damaged," he'd told me earlier, nodding in the direction of the bowler hat on Sonny's head and the vintage military frock coat that Kennedy had on.)

"Yes, of *course* you can do it, Sadie," Kyle told me firmly now, as he continued dab-dab-dabbing his brush. "Just imagine you're on a street in New York instead of here, and in a video for . . . for . . . *which* type of music do you like?"

I liked loads of different kinds of music: old rock stuff my dad had got me into, and newer, indie-ish stuff too.

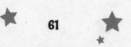

"Um, there's a band called The Drop Zone who are really good," I mumbled, scared to move in case I ended up with brown eyeshadow on my nose or something.

"Well, *there* you go. Just pretend you're in the video for a *proper* band, instead of *this* lot. . ."

I grinned, loving the fact that Kyle's sense of humour was even more sarcastic than mine.

Don't get me wrong; it wasn't as if I was big buddies with him (Kyle was in his twenties, and hung out with models, for goodness' sake), but it felt like there was someone on my side – someone ready to try and talk me out of the ridiculous trembling fit I was having.

Hannah and Letitia were helping as well, although I could have done without them both wearing "Sadie Rocks" T-shirts, handed out by – eek! – Angie the record company publicity girl, who I'd managed to avoid talking to so far. ("Hi! How *are* you? So you're going out with my dad? Brilliant! By the way, isn't he *nearly* old enough to be *your* dad too?")

Whatever, I'd forced myself to ignore the T-shirts and look at Letty and Hannah from the neck up only, which worked OK. We'd hung out together, while the morning began with Sonny and the boys miming and posing along to a section of their single, which was blasting out of some tinny CD player. (The proper, studio-perfect track would be added in later, so that anyone watching the finished video – like who?! – wouldn't hear the beeping horns of passing cars and the lairy swearing from blokes in white vans.)

And of course, there was Cormac, who'd come to the shoot to cheer on Sonny, but ended up giving *me* a pep talk after my first disastrous rehearsal. All I'd had to do was stroll along the pavement "casually", while the boys danced and pranced around me, but I'd pretty much managed to quake my way along like a malfunctioning robot who was about to throw up.

"*Next* time, just try looking at a point straight ahead," he'd told me, just before Kyle grabbed me for (make-up) touch-ups. "Take lots of slow, deep breaths, and walk slowly too. Like a cat striding along a wall."

That *last* bit hadn't worked for me; this morning as I was leaving the house, I'd watched Dog wobbling along the tall fence between our garden and our neighbour's. She was as elegant as a pig on a tightrope. Then she'd had a sneezing fit and fallen sideways into next door's hydrangeas.

I quickly shook that image out of my head and

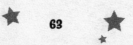

looked at Cormac instead. He was a bit of a cartoon character in lots of ways – tall, skinny, luminous orange hair and milk-white skin with a tendency to blushing – but that black funeral suit he wore had a habit of sobering you up super-quick.

Taking his advice, I imagined myself inhaling and exhaling deep, slow breaths, and walking at an unhurried snail's pace. I could just picture him doing the very same thing as he strode respectfully behind a coffin. . .

Yep, I'd try and keep that in my head. It was a pretty appropriate image, after all; I mean, if anyone from school ever saw this video, I'd probably be dead anyway.

"OK, Sadie," came a confident voice. It belonged to Richie the director. He rubbed his artfully grown stubble and stared at me as if he was deeply regretting getting me in to do my novelty cameo role. "Let's try it for *real* this time."

I tried to concentrate on what he was saying, but it was hard. For a start – despite Cormac's pep talk and Kyle's jokes – my stomach was so crunched up in nervous knots that I felt like I was going to cave in on myself. Plus I'd spotted a worrying new development out of the corner of my eye; Hannah's smiley mum had just arrived, all a-twitter to watch the filming – with *Harry* in tow.

Please *no*. . .! Younger siblings were fine, if they were cute and puppyish like Charonna or Martha, *not* if they were venomous and deadly like Harry.

"Now what I want from you, Sadie, is to consider your *motivation* here," prattled Richie.

What? I didn't *have* any motivation. I just had that nervy knot of dread in my stomach. . .

"Just before you start walking, I want you to think, who *is* Sadie?! And why *does* she rock? Yeah?"

"Uh, OK," I mumbled, though I really wanted to say, "Er, what are you on about?"

"Great! Then once you've worked it out, I want you to forget it all! Wipe it from your mind!!" Richie carried on excitedly, wafting his hand through the air, as if he was erasing my memory. "Just say to yourself, *I* am Sadie! And I *rock*! Hold that dynamic image in your head and *go* for it! Do you get me? Great!"

"Do all directors talk like that?" I whispered to Kyle, as Richie strode off self-importantly. He'd reminded me of the presenters on the shopping channels, saying a zillion overblown words in a row, when really "Could you try it again, please?" would have done.

"Plenty of them do," Kyle answered with a shrug, as he applied a slick of clear lipgloss. "But don't be intimidated by him. Just imagine him in his pants – that's what *I* usually do when people try to boss me about."

CLAP, CLAP, CLAP!!

Richie was slapping his hands together, trying to get everyone's attention. Instantly, I did as Kyle said and tried imagining him in his pants; in my head, they were Spider-Man ones, the same as Kennedy's had been that time his shorts split.

"Positions, everyone!!" Richie barked.

Uh-oh – the cameras were nearly ready to roll for real. (Help. . .)

"OK, you're done," announced Kyle, standing back and shooing me off. "Go! Think New York! Think Drop Zone!"

I tried, I really did.

I started walking towards Sonny (bowler hat, *my* stripy T-shirt, jeans, guitar slung across his chest); Hal (trilby, denim jacket, skater shorts); Marcus (beanie hat, long-sleeved orange top, baggy white decorator's dungarees); Ziggy (ear-flapper woolly hat, doctor-style blue cotton trousers, red-and-white Hawaiian shirt lent by Dad); and Kennedy (the vintage military frock coat, combats, plate face).

Breathe slowly, walk slowly, I coached myself, hoping my lips weren't moving. *Just get yourself over to them, wait for the director to shout "Action", and then everything will be OK. . .*

And it *was* OK, for two whole seconds, till I went *flying*.

I mean, *one* minute, I was headed towards Sonny and Co. and upright (ideal).

The *next*, I'd been thunked hard by something on the left side of my legs, and found myself plonked on to a . . . *whatever*, hurtling towards the band at high speed, leaning at a forty-five-degree angle (definitely *not* ideal).

"HARRY!" I heard Hannah yell in shock.

"Harry! Stop right now! Put Sadie DOWN!!" I heard Hannah's mum call out.

"Oi!" shouted a man from the doorway of the office shop, as I whizzed by on what I realized must have been one of his whirly-wheeled multicoloured office chairs.

"HA HA HA HA HA!" I heard Kennedy Plate-Face Watson laugh louder than anybody else, as I sped on a collision course towards Sonny and the boys.

"Brilliant, ha ha!" I was pretty sure I heard Richie the director cackle.

Grrr. . .

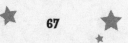

Five minutes later, I'd stopped feeling sick. (Travel sick? Sick from the shame?)

Harry – who'd thought stealing a whirly-wheeled chair and scooping me up in it was the best idea in the world – had been dragged home by his mum, who was last heard threatening to stop his pocket money till he was thirty, at *least*.

Stuff that had *also* happened in the last five minutes: Kyle had added some more make-up, to hide the white-from-fright and blush-pink-from-embarrassment glare radiating from my face; and Richie the director had spent that time in a huddle with the boys, telling them what *their* motivation was, probably.

"Good to go again, Sadie?" Richie called out, turning away from the lads towards me.

"Yes," I muttered in a very small, very reluctant voice. I wanted to go, for sure. I wanted to go straight home and crawl under the covers in the Trash Pad and never come out again.

But as I couldn't exactly do that, I did as I was told and got into position.

Just stroll, I ordered myself. *Look into the distance; take deep, slow breaths; don't think of Dog falling off the fence this morning; ignore the beardy bloke in the Spider-Man underpants; and pretend I'm in New York. . .*

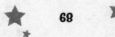

Easy.

Not.

"And . . . *action!*" snapped Richie from somewhere up ahead, though I was so busy focusing on a red postbox in the distance, I couldn't have told you where he was.

Tinny music began pounding out as best as it could from the feeble portable CD player. I started walking. I could sense the boys in their ridiculous clothes doing some ridiculous dance all around me, but I forced myself to blank them out and stare haughtily at the postbox.

Yay – I wasn't shaking. I didn't feel quite so much like a malfunctioning robot who was about to throw up. Maybe this was going to be all ri—

"AAAAAA-YEEEEEEEEEE!!" someone called out, who just happened to be *me.*

Not *again!* I'd been hijacked by a whirly-wheeled office chair, *this* time, I realized, by members of Sonny's stupid band, and *this* time because Richie the director had *told* them to. *That's* what that last, pre-camera-rolling huddle had been all about!

As I zoomed at high speed along the pavement, pushed by five deeply idiotic boys, I saw several stunned faces whiz by (Angie's, Cormac's, Hannah's and Charonna's), and then Letitia's –

though *her* gaze seemed to be on someone else and not me (weird, in the circumstances).

Next, the postbox I'd been focusing on loomed up.

Whoosh! We were past it, and somewhere behind us a delighted voice yelled, "CUT! It's a wrap! Well done, everybody! Well done, Sadie – you're a good sport!!"

Yeah, and you're as weaselly as Harry, I thought bleakly about Richie the director.

As the whirly-wheeled office chair began to lose momentum, the five sniggering, breathless boys let go of it, allowing it to whirl to a standstill.

Above the sound of my furiously pounding heart, I suddenly realized something slightly startling.

For the merest millisecond there, I'd seen a glimpse of a face peeking out from behind the red postbox.

It was a face I didn't know very well; a face I'd seen only twice, from a distance. Once was from Dad's flat, looking down, as *she* looked up, and the second time was outside our house, right before Nonna went charging out with a bucket and mop with orders to clean up the chalked messages she'd left for Sonny and the band.

Oh, yes, that barely glimpsed face belonged to a teenage girl called Mel.

It seemed like the band's mad stalker fan was back, back, *back*. . .

7

Welcome to shopping hell

Mum chose her wedding dress less than a minute into our shopping trip.

We'd taken the bus to the N1 shopping centre, just down the road from us in Islington, and blam! – while Nonna and Gran were still gawping around deciding where to start first – Mum spotted the most beautiful dress in the window of Oasis and knew she'd found The One.

It was made of gorgeous, shimmery satin, in a kind of silvery/mauve/grey colour, a bit like pigeons' feathers or oil on a puddle (hey, you know what I mean).

It had thin straps and these diagonal seams that swirled around her like the slide on the old-fashioned helter-skelter featured in the Twits video.

"It's just *lovely*, Nicola," Gran sighed, all twinkly-eyed, when Mum came out of the changing rooms to give us a twirl.

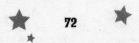

"I like the way it swings out when you swivel," I told Mum.

"That's because of the way it's *cut*, Sadie," said Nonna knowledgeably. "That style is called an empire line."

I could tell from Gran's tight-lipped mouth that it wasn't, but I had the feeling that she was trying very hard not to start bickering this early into our outing. Luckily, someone *else* set Nonna straight.

"Um, it's *not* an empire line cut, actually," said the shop assistant, brushing by with an armload of clothes to put on the rails. "It's a bias cut!"

"Really? Well, thank you!" Nonna smiled warmly as the shop assistant bustled off. Then she dropped her voice and muttered, "Don't want to embarrass the girl, but it's *definitely* empire line!"

Mum gave a quick, despairing roll of her eyes, and headed back to the changing room to get out of the dress.

"It's a *gorgeous* frock, whatever the cut," said Gran diplomatically, watching as the back of the dress trailed along the ground like a rippling North Sea wave.

"Yes, it is," agreed Nonna. "Though I'm not sure about the colour and how appropriate it is to get *married* in. You *do* know that grey is the colour of mourning in India, don't you?"

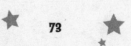

Gran's mouth pursed up again, and I saw her nostrils flare. We'd already heard my borderline-mad Nonna tell us with great certainty on the bus down here that white bread was actually *much* more nutritious than wholegrain; that she'd read a report in the paper that sheep were in danger of extinction in the next ten years; and that in certain lights, Martha was the *spitting* image of Princess Diana (um, Martha was cute, but how a plump, wispy-haired baby could resemble a tall, blonde, dead princess was anyone's guess).

"Actually, *white's* the colour of mourning in India," I couldn't help myself saying, even though I knew it could start a very, *very* pointless debate.

"Sadie, dear, I think you'll find—"

Nonna tilted her head to the side and put on her most patronizing voice as she began to (wrongly) correct me.

"Well, even if grey *was* the colour of mourning in India," I interrupted quickly, trying to keep calm, "it wouldn't matter, because Mum and Will are getting married in *London*!"

I'd like to use the excuse that I was getting more wound up by Nonna than usual thanks to my very early morning schedule and the draining horror of the video shoot. But really, it was just because of Nonna.

And if she'd already begun doing my head in at the very *start* of our shopping trip, you can imagine how I felt four stores and one hour later.

"Mum," I mumbled, putting a hand on top of my head to stop it from exploding. "*Please* say I don't have to wear a dress like one of these, with tights and smart shoes and everything. . ."

The hand that *wasn't* holding my head on was reluctantly clutching five hangers, with five *awful*, floaty, girly dresses dangling from them, all chosen for me by Nonna. I'd ignored the rhinestone-encrusted, patent-black, high-heeled sandals that she'd tried to point out to me a minute ago.

"Hey, look – she's been sidetracked by shiny stuff," whispered Mum, nodding towards Nonna, who was studying something spangly on a rail while she thought I was heading for the changing rooms. A few rails further down, I noticed, Gran had her specs on and was frowning at price tags. "Dump those, Sadie, and let me grab something I think you'll like while she's not looking. . ."

I felt my shoulders sag with relief. If I heard just *one* more time how I needed to disguise my round shoulders/stop slouching/dress more like a young lady should/take pride in my appearance, even if my figure hadn't really developed properly, I'd be just about ready to shove one of these chic wooden hangers right inside my tactless Nonna's mouth, and risk going to jail for granny-bashing.

As for Mum – she could sometimes be a bit ditzy (specially if she was lost in some plinky-plonky classical music piece), but boy did I love her. And I loved what she got me. Looking in the changing-room mirror, I saw a dress, but a short one: a heather purple smock-style number with little puff sleeves and a subtle rose on the right-hand side, made out of the same material. It went fine with the black leggings and dark-purple suede ballet pumps Mum had picked out.

But I didn't step out of the cubicle and give Mum a twirl; instead, I quickly slithered out of everything, yanked on my lived-in jeans, T-shirt and trainers, and scrunched my wedding stuff into a tight pile. My plan was to thrust it all into Mum's arms the second I got out – i.e., giving Nonna the *least* opportunity to spot the clothes and criticize them before Mum got to the till.

But even before I swished the cubicle curtain back, I could hear that Nonna was slightly preoccupied anyway.

"Joan, you're being ridiculous! We can't *both* try on the same outfit!" she was snapping.

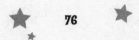

"I didn't say we should, *Muriel*!" Gran snapped back, using Nonna's much-hated original name. "But since I was in the queue for the changing room first, I think we both know who should have the right to *choose* it!"

"But come *on*, Joan! Be practical! With your pale Celtic colouring, you're going to look completely washed out in this delicate green. Whereas with *my* tan –"

I hurried out of the changing room to see Nonna and Gran doing a stand-off, both holding silky peppermint dresses with matching bolero jackets.

I could *also* see my mum staring at the ceiling, as if she was hoping that God or a thunderbolt might intervene in the latest round of the Granny Wars.

"– it's just perfect. Can't you see that? Hmmm?" Nonna finished, holding the dress up against her.

Uh-oh. People were beginning to stare, enjoying the spectacle of two nanas having a ding-dong. Usually, when Nonna and Gran started, Sonny would leap in and distract them with some jazz dance moves, or burst into a chorus from his latest song, or just be their all-round golden-boy grandson.

But he wasn't here, and their untalented

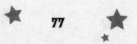

granddaughter growling, "Would you two grow up?" probably wouldn't have the same soothing effect.

Mum must have spotted my face falling.

"Sadie, do you want to go and have a wander round the CD shop across the way? I'll sort these two out and I'll ring your mobile when it's safe to come meet us. . ."

I wanted to give Mum a big hug to say thank you for letting me escape, but doing that would have meant staying for an extra couple of seconds in the vicinity of the seriously sniping grannies.

So I bolted (with gratitude). . .

Over in the giant CD store, Saturday-afternoon shoppers swarmed, checking out albums and computer games and magazines, while deafening, chest-thumping rap music thudded from random speakers and matching visuals on the giant video screens above the "Pay Here" desks.

But for me, it felt as calm as a sun-kissed desert island after the shenanigans with my grandmothers.

I shot a look out of the plate-glass window over towards the clothes shop they were still in with Mum, half-expecting to see Gran and Nonna being escorted out by the security guard for breach of the peace, or come tumbling out in a wrestling tussle, hitting each other over the head with their handbags. . .

My left hip suddenly began to wobble slightly – I forgot I'd set my messages to vibrate during the video shoot this morning.

Flipping my mobile out of my jeans pocket, I spotted two text messages from Letitia.

This morning was great, wasn't it? L x

Um, well, it might have been for her. *She* wasn't the one being humiliated, first by a weaselly boy and then on film for all the world to see. *She* wasn't the one with bruises on the back of her thighs from collisions with whirly-wheeled office chairs.

Didn't K look amazing?

K? Who or what is K? I thought to myself, as I wandered along the "D" (for Drop Zone) section of the CD racks.

What are you on about? I texted her, remembering now how she had looked straight past me this morning during my hurtle of shame. What had she been gawping at that was more interesting than her best friend's mortification? Mind you, it was hard to figure out the inner workings of Letty's fluff-filled brain sometimes.

Remember how she got in a jealous huff when I

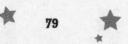

bought Cormac a present not so long ago? I reminded myself. The present had been a small book about the cemeteries of London. I thought he'd love it, but the same day, Sonny blew my gift out of the water by promising to hook Cormac up with that Martin Shore comedian guy. (Which – no surprise – had never happened.)

The joke was, of course, that Letty was miffed with me for giving a pressie to her Fantasy Boyfriend — i.e., the Fantasy Boyfriend who didn't even *know* he was her Fantasy Boyfriend.

Kennedy – duh!! a text immediately pinged back.

Too right, *duh*!

Now I got it! *Now* I understood why Letty had been gazing longingly over my shoulder while I'd gritted my teeth and flown by her in a blur of whirly wheels and green-tweedy upholstery.

Cormac had passed his sell-by date as her current crush. He'd been dumped (though he'd never know it) – for Sonny's plate-faced mate!

Wow, that was funny. And how many *other* girls were going to fall for wide-faced, big-headed, pea-brained Kennedy Watson once the Sadie Rocks video and single were out there?

Speaking of cheesy boy-band lead singers, I could hear one right now.

"*Just wanna hold your hand, girl! It would mean everything to meeeeeee. . .*"

The Twits. They'd replaced the previous tough rap band who'd been up on the giant video screens; the one whose members looked mean enough to eat squeaky clean pretty boys like Benjii and Co. for breakfast.

"*Ooooh, say you will, girl, say you will, girl!*"

Sonny would hate to see this. He'd be hurtling copies of random CDs at the screen if he was here, and would end up locked in a police cell with other troublemakers like Nonna and Gran.

"Ooof!"

Yikes. The combination of being distracted and walking meant I'd thumped straight into a stationary shopper.

"Oh, sorry!" I apologized to the teenage girl I'd rammed.

"Oh . . . hello!" said the girl.

It was the same face I'd seen peeking out from behind the postbox this morning at 8.05 a.m. It was Mel the mad fan stalker. My first instinct was to run, but before I could, she spoke again.

"They're nowhere *near* as good as Sadie Rocks, are they?" Mel suddenly blurted, as if we knew each other in an ordinary way, instead of a deeply weird way.

What could I say? Choosing between Sadie Rocks and The Twits was like having to choose between getting a Chinese burn or eating a toothpaste sandwich. I mean, I'd much rather choose neither.

"Well, I. . ."

Mel didn't seem that interested in whatever I was going to reply. I guess she took it as read that since my name was Sadie, I was related to someone in the band *and* I'd been in their video that my vote would automatically go to Sonny's band. *Ha*.

"I'm here to pre-order the 'We Are Family' single!" Mel burbled on excitedly. "It's out next Friday!"

"Yeah, I know," I said, feeling awkward to be in the presence of an older, fifteen-year-old girl whose hobby seemed to be spying on my brother and his friends. I mean, how had she come to know about the filming of the video in the first place?

"Actually, I'm going to order *three* copies, just to help them get higher in the charts!" she added, her dark eyes glinting with mad fan mania.

"Wow. . ." I muttered dubiously.

"And I might buy some more copies during the week, if I get an advance on my pocket money," Mel said, sounding enthusiastic and bonkers, before changing the subject. "Kennedy's so cute, isn't he?"

Um, no, I felt like saying. His favourite type of humour was fart jokes and he ate with his mouth open, so you could see his lunch revolving round like it was in the drum of a washing machine. No matter how soft-focus and dreamy the video ended up making him look, I knew I could never think of Kennedy as anything else but my brother's dumb, dorky mate.

"And it was *so* sweet of him to text me and tell me where the shoot was happening."

Aha. Kennedy had promised the rest of the lads that he wouldn't have anything to do with Mel again, not after he admitted that *he'd* been the one who told her where everyone in the band *lived*, which had naturally spooked them all out.

"Yeah, he's a *real* sweetie," I droned.

Yeah, a real sweetie with a big ego, who couldn't resist his ego being massaged even *more* by having a real live mega-fan trailing after them adoringly.

Maybe it was the sarcasm in my voice, or the snarl on my face (I can't help it – my lopsided smile *always* ends up looking like a snarl), but Mel sort of sensed I was as wary of her as a sardine being circled by a shark.

"I'm not a weird stalker or something!" she said

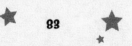

hurriedly. "I know the other boys might still think I am, but—"

Mel's dark eyes widened, spotting something terrifying behind me.

I flipped round, and saw . . . Nonna, breezing into the store like a battleship, her eyes casting around for me (well, she sure hadn't come in for a Snoop Dogg CD).

"Sadie! Oh, *SADIEEEEEEEE*!" she yoo-hoo'd across the shop floor at me. "We're ready to go now!!"

I turned to see Mel's reaction – after all, Nonna was her nemesis, the person who'd chased her off the premises and put a stop (till now) to her fan mania.

But she had vanished into thin air, like the now-she's-here-now-she's-gone stalker that she was. . .

Sadie's Socks

Dogs panted in the warm sunshine and scratched at their fleas.

Their owners, meanwhile, tittered and clapped.

It's not exactly the normal dog-walking experience you might come across in your local park, but it was in mine this Sunday morning.

Cormac was standing on his upturned wooden crate, doing his comedy routine for a crowd that included dogs and dog owners, plus me, Hannah, Letty, Sonny and Kennedy.

He'd done it quite a few times now, and the Sunday-morning crowds were getting bigger, maybe now that people were passing the word around about the strange, skinny, redheaded boy in the funeral suit who sometimes just turned up and busked funny stuff on a box for free.

Who knows, maybe they were disappointed when they wandered down to Highbury Fields with their little Fifis and big Barneys and found it

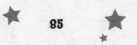

was one of the days Cormac *wasn't* out practising his comedy routine. . .

Still, this Sunday was turning out to be another success, with lots of laughs happening for Cormac (phew). The only things that were different were a) Dad hadn't turned up, and b) Letty was staring doe-eyed at Kennedy instead of Cormac.

"Hey, is it my imagination, or is Letty practically *drooling* over Kennedy?" asked Hannah, as we crowded into the small ladies' loos of the café we'd come to after the *Cormac McConnell live at Highbury Fields!* show.

"It's not your imagination," I said, feeling a bit queasy.

I wasn't so much queasy about Letty having a crush on dopey old Kennedy; I was more squeamish 'cause Sonny had just told me Dad had been out on another date with *Angie* last night. She'd mentioned it to Sonny yesterday at the shoot. She hadn't mentioned it to *me*, mainly 'cause in-between quaking with nerves and being hijacked by chairs, I'd managed to avoid even catching her eye, never mind being close enough to have a girly chat.

"That is *gross*," mumbled Hannah, from the second of the two cubicles.

True, I thought to myself, idly looking at

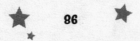

the graffiti on the back of the door to my cubicle.

"You *do* know that Letty's only got a crush on him because he's the lead singer of the band, don't you?" Hannah asked flatly.

"Well, *yeah*," I semi-agreed. I mean, it was kind of pointless trying to make sense of Letty's pretend love life. She once had a two-month crush on a boy pictured on the back of a cereal box, for goodness' sake.

Swoosh, went the flush on Hannah's side.

"I mean, it's not like Letty's ever paid him any attention before, has she?" Hannah prattled on outside as she washed her hands. "Anytime she met him round at your house, it's not as if. . ."

I sort of tuned out at that point, slightly bored with hearing Hannah bad-mouth her rival best friend. Instead, I gazed at the graffiti on the back of my cubicle door. There were four *K8 4 Jez* type lovey-dovey messages, a couple of swear words, one rude joke I didn't get, and two names of bands.

Wow. Maybe Sonny's band would be famous enough one day to have girl vandals scratch their name on toilet doors. Actually, come to think of it, Mel had probably already started.

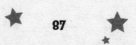

And speaking of Mel, there was someone I needed to have a word with about that. . .

"Oi!" I said, sliding back into my seat around the table and slapping my hand down beside Kennedy.

Kennedy ignored me. He was hunched over a serviette, writing something down with what looked like Letty's favourite Nearly Black eyeliner pencil.

"Hey, Sadie; we're just trying to work out stuff like what The Twist have got that we haven't," Sonny explained, pointing at two columns of scribbles with a line down the middle. At the top of the second column, it read *Sadie's Socks*, or at least it looked a lot like that with Kennedy's scrawl in the blunt eyeliner.

The Twits and Sadie's Socks . . . perfect.

"Have you talked to him about Mel?" I asked Sonny, while pointing at Kennedy's head.

Yesterday tea time, I'd thought Sonny would have been open-mouthed when I told him about their little stalker buddy hiding out behind the postbox, and about me slamming into her in the CD store.

I'd thought after that he'd be *raring* to go round to Kennedy's and rant at him for being in contact with Mel.

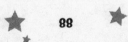

But Sonny had been annoyingly texting while I talked, and I knew he was only half paying attention. Specially when I tested my theory with a lie and announced that there'd just been a newsflash on our mini TV about his stage school burning down. (That got a distracted grunt and a mindless "Uh-huh?")

"Oh, yeah. . .!" Sonny said, now that he'd scanned his glitter-spangled memory banks and vaguely remembered our conversation. "Kennedy – Sadie told me you've been texting that mad girl about what we're up to!"

"Yeah, I did that," Kennedy mumbled, while writing *Better lead singer* in the Sadie's Socks column. "Sorry."

"Uh. OK." Sonny shrugged. "Hey, Kennedy, you should write *They're fifteen and we're only thirteen*, 'cause really, that means The Twist will get the older teenage girl fans that we won't."

Excuse me? That was *it*? That was as much of a shouting down as my brother was going to give his mate?!

"Wait a minute! She's *nuts*! Have you forgotten that she totally freaked all the other lads out when she turned up at their houses?!" I reminded Kennedy in particular, and Sonny too, while I was at it.

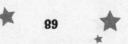

89

"Yeah, but I was thinking about it and I *sort* of think that I think she's OK now," said Kennedy, making very little sense, in a startlingly ungrammatical way. "And, y'know, we're going to have to get used to having thousands of fans hanging around and going mad for us. It's just the way it's going to be. . ."

I gasped at the sheer cockiness of Kennedy Watson.

Other reactions round the table? Well, I noticed Hannah raise her eyebrows, but more like she was *impressed*, rather than shocked. Letty fluttered her eyelashes at Kennedy's splendidness, and Sonny gave a slow nod of agreement.

Cormac's face seemed very straight, very unreadable.

"And think of all the paparazzi that'll be trailing you – don't forget them!" he suddenly said, giving me the quickest of winks.

Phew. . . I might be losing my best friends to the Dark Side, but at least Cormac was in wind-up mode.

"Too right there'll be paparazzi!" muttered Kennedy, oblivious to the fact that Cormac was taking the mick.

"Ooh, will you get to go to film premieres and stuff, d'you reckon?" asked Hannah, tucking her long brown hair behind her ears, all the better to hear more tales of the celebrity whirlwind that Kennedy was sure they'd be sucked up into.

"Hey, it's all part of it!" Kennedy shrugged, sounding supremely confident. "That's the fame game!"

Urgh. . . Not only did he sound like he had an ego the size of the *universe*, he also sounded like the middle-aged presenter of some corny TV quiz show!

"I got another one for the list!" Sonny suddenly burst out. "Put down *Video and single out a week earlier* on The Twist's list. We'll find out later today how high they get in the charts!"

"Yeah, but even if they make number one, so will *you* guys!" said Letty, supportively.

"Absolutely!" Hannah chipped in.

Yikes.

I stared at my two best friends, pleased that they agreed about something for a change, but worrying that they were starting to sound a little like mad stalker fans themselves.

"*I close my eyes*. . ." warbled a tinny, digital voice from Sonny's phone. His new ringtone, from *Joseph and the Amazing Technicolour Dreamcoat*.

"Hello?" he bellowed into it. "Yep – that's it. OK, see you a minute!"

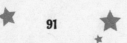

"Who's that – your new mate *Mel*?" I teased him.

"Nope – just someone I was texting last night. You'll see in a minute!" he said, with an annoyingly secretive smile suddenly creeping across his face.

I dreaded to think. It would probably be a journalist from a girls' magazine, or someone who was interested in running the Sadie's Socks Fan Club, I bet.

Whoever it was, I was well and truly fed up of Sonny and Kennedy's dumb band being the *only* thing we could talk about.

"Hey, Cormac – there seemed to be *loads* more people listening to you in the park today!" I said, swizzling the conversation around, and thinking of dogs (and therefore owners) I hadn't seen on previous Sundays.

"Yeah, it was . . . pretty good!" Cormac agreed, but with a slight, sweet blush on his pale cheeks. (Sonny and Kennedy *never* blushed, mainly 'cause of the powerful force field of cockiness surrounding them at all times.)

"So what about doing a *proper* show somewhere?" Hannah asked him, thankfully joining in with this alternative natter. "You've got lots of really funny stuff to talk about now!"

"Nah, I don't think I'm ready for that yet. . ." said Cormac shyly, hunching himself over his juice, which was the same shade as his hair.

"WRONG!" said someone loudly, bounding into the café and standing by our table.

Get me: I started to get up to go, thinking it was a waiter come to tell us we were sitting at a table that was reserved or something. (Duh. . .)

"You were *great* today!" the young man – who wasn't actually *dressed* like a waiter – announced.

Apart from wearing jeans and a T-shirt with a big question mark on it, he also had a scruffy bearded collie at the end of a lead. Now, waiters definitely *didn't* come to take your order or shoo you off a reserved table with a dog in tow. . .

"Hey, guys! *This*," boomed Sonny, standing up next to the guy in jeans with the dog, "is *only* Martin Shore!"

Martin Shore gave the rest of us a hi-but-I-really-don't-need-to-know-who-you-lot-are smile, and stuck his hand out towards Cormac.

"Sonny's been on my case, trying to get me to come along today to hear your stuff, Cormac – and I'm glad I did!" said the floppy-haired, almost-famous comedian who was a former student at Sonny's stage school. "It blew me away! I wish I'd had a routine like that when *I* was seventeen!"

"Did you . . . I mean, did you really like it?" Cormac asked hesitantly. He was as pink as a very embarrassed prawn now.

"Yeah, *totally*!" raved Martin Shore, pulling a chair out and sitting down beside Cormac, while his dog started sniffing under the table. It seemed especially interested in my trainers. Maybe they smelled intriguingly of Dog (the cat), or *more* intriguingly, rabbit (of the house variety). Or maybe they just smelled of feet.

Whatever, as Martin Shore yakked and his scruffy dog sniffed, Hannah and Letty (and me, I admit) watched slightly wide-eyed and open-mouthed as this sort-of-famous bloke made our friend an offer he couldn't refuse.

"Listen, how do you fancy being the first act on at my opening showcase in the West End next week?"

As Cormac gave a choked "Yes!" and Martin Shore started firing details at him, I shot a look at Sonny.

Yeah, it was brilliant of my brother to have arranged this even-better-than-expected get-together, but – actual fact – he *wouldn't* have if I hadn't guilt-tripped him into remembering he'd offered to do it in the first place.

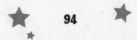

"Sorry! No dogs allowed, please!!" a genuine waiter suddenly bustled up and announced.

Quick as a flash, Martin Shore:

a) gave the waiter a charming apology
b) handed Cormac a business card and told him to call him
c) gave the rest of us a bye-whoever-you-are smile, and. . .
d) disappeared out of the café door with his hairy hound.

"Wow! *Cheers*, Sonny!" said Cormac, with a look of stunned gratitude on his face.

"Hey, if it hadn't been for Sadie reminding me of my promise the other night, it might never have happened!" Sonny DIDN'T say.

"Whatever!" Sonny said instead, with mock casualness.

And *that* was when I sussed that it was all about Sonny again, just like it always was.

Just like at home, when I got reasonably good marks for tests and a mild well-done from my parents, while *Sonny* got a stand-up ovation from them when we went to see his end-of-term plays.

Just like Nonna and Gran would "oooh!" and

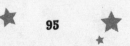

"aahhhh!" as Sonny demonstrated a new high-kicking dance routine he'd learned, while they'd mention to *me* that the label was sticking out of the back of my top.

Honestly, it was enough to make a girl go and join the Twits' Fan Club straight away. . .

9

Memories of meringues. . .

O-*kaaaayyyy*. . .

Now *that* wasn't something I expected to see when I walked in the living room.

"Looks great!" Dad was nodding as Mum held her wedding dress up against herself and spun around. "It's a lot less . . . puffy and fluffy than the one you wore to *our* wedding!"

I'd just come from the café in the park, where a *nearly*-famous person called Martin had made Cormac's day. And here was a *not*-famous person often *called* Martin (wrongly, by Nonna) giving compliments to his wife on the dress she was going to wear when she married her next husband.

"Oi! How dare you take the mickey out of that dress, Max! I *loved* it!" Mum laughed at Dad's cheek.

"What?! I *liked* it – at the time! It was very nice, Nicky . . . for a *meringue*!"

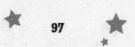

"Ooh!" gasped Mum. "Well, I don't suppose you'd *quite* fit into your wedding suit these days, not with the pizza and beer diet you've been on the last few years!"

They hadn't even noticed me hovering in the doorway, they were so busy teasing each other rotten.

"I'll have you know I eat very healthily these days!" Dad retorted, patting his round fuzzy tummy, which was thankfully under wraps in today's particular shirt.

"Yes – which is all down to Joan staying with you and cooking all your meals!" Mum giggled. "I hope you're paying your poor mother for her catering services, since you expect her to feed you every night!"

"Not *every* night!" Dad corrected her. "I went out to dinner yesterday, to the Iznik!"

"Did you?" asked Mum, still smiling, but looking a bit puzzled. The Turkish restaurant in Highbury was our favourite place to go as a family. But since me and Sonny had been mooching round the house last night, I guess she was wondering *who* exactly Dad had had dinner with.

"Uh-huh! I had a date!" Dad announced brightly. Ahhh . . . was this payback time? Was Dad trying to get Mum *jealous* here?

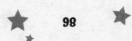

"A date! Well, I think you'd better tell me more!" Mum said, raising her eyebrows at Dad.

(She didn't seem in any way jealous; just surprised and intrigued. Nice try, Dad.)

"It's Angie – from the record company!" said Dad, acting very pleased with himself.

"The skinny publicity girl?" Mum checked. "Isn't she a bit young for you, Max?"

"She's not *that* young! She's thirty this month!" Dad protested.

Ah, so Dad wasn't *quite* old enough to be her father. But finding out Angie's age didn't make me feel any better about her dating Dad. Not when I was certain – sure as Dog was a cat – that Angie was nothing but a rebound girlfriend, to make Dad feel better (seemed to be working) and Mum feel jealous (definitely *not* working).

"YAY!! Dad, you fixed the TV! Amazing!!" yelped Sonny, pushing noisily past me into the living room. I'd left him behind a few minutes ago, saying his fond farewells to Kennedy (the idiot). He'd only just got in. "Go, Dad, go!"

As Sonny pounded the air, I noticed what I hadn't noticed before – our big telly was back in place, with some shopping-channel presenter on mute, showing off a moisturizer that was made of the nectar of honey blossom and spun gold,

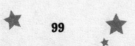

probably. Sitting on the floor beside the mega-telly was the diddy portable, unplugged, blank-screened and forlorn.

"Yep, your dad popped round with a new cable, so we're back in business!" Mum beamed at Sonny.

"You mean, we'll now be forced to watch endless repeats of *A Place In The Sun* in widescreen," I joked bleakly, wandering further into the room and parking myself down on the sofa. A small, disgruntled rabbit – which I'd mistaken for a cushion – bounced up at the other end of the sofa. (At least I wasn't within nipping distance.)

"What? What are you saying about *A Place In The Sun*? Is it on?" we all heard Nonna's voice call from the stairs, only to get ever louder as she thudded down to join us.

"No – it's just that Max is here and has fixed up the TV for us," Mum explained to Nonna, who'd sailed into the room in a floor-length, wine-coloured bathrobe and with a scarlet towel wrapped round her head. She had obviously just come out of the bath or shower, but looked more like she should be wedged to the prow of an old sailing ship.

"I was just saying we can all watch our favourite

programmes on it now," I fibbed lightly, which made Sonny snort.

"Super!" said Nonna, gazing at the shopping-channel presenter, who was chattering silently and massaging moisturizer into her face.

I noticed Nonna was holding a pile of clothes destined for the laundry basket. Not that she would be the one *doing* her laundry, since she seemed allergic to all kinds of housework. Even *Clyde* did more than her. At least he got rid of stray crumbs on the floor in a very effective manner. (Nibble, nibble, *burp*.)

"But what on earth are you doing, Nicola, dear?" Nonna was suddenly frowning at Mum, as if Mum was a naughty kid caught smearing her mother's lipstick all over her face.

"Well . . . I was just showing Max the dress I bought yesterday," Mum said hesitantly, knowing that Nonna would have *something* to say about that.

"Well, that's not lucky, not lucky at *all*!" muttered Nonna.

Dad and Sonny looked confused. But I knew what she was trying to get at. She'd just got her superstitions in a muddle, naturally.

"Nonna, it's supposed to be unlucky for a bride to show the *groom* her wedding dress. It

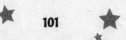

doesn't count if it's the previous husband!" I told her.

"I think you'll find that it's *any* husband, Sadie, dear," Nonna infuriatingly tried to correct me.

"Hey! That reminds me, Nicky!" Dad suddenly said brightly. "Did you get your Decree Absolute through? Mine came yesterday!"

Decree Absolute? It sounded like some kind of blue-coloured cocktail. But what was it again? Sonny was as clueless as I was, I could tell from his confused expression.

"Um, no!" Mum said, looking quite startled. "But then I think there's a pile of post on the kitchen table that I haven't had a chance to go through yet. It's probably there. . ."

"Well! You two are now officially divorced! Congratulations!" Nonna announced, suddenly making the situation crystal clear to us clueless twins.

How strange.

I mean, Mum and Dad had been apart for nearly three and a half years now, but knowing they were properly, completely and *forever* divorced . . . well, it sort of *hurt* a bit, weirdly.

It felt strange to my parents too, you could tell from the way they laughed too loud and shrugged shyly at each other.

"Thank *goodness*!" gasped Nonna, in a very theatrical manner. "I was worried it wouldn't come through in time and you'd have to cancel the wedding! Then I'd *never* get a chance to wear that lovely peppermint-green outfit I bought! Do you want me to bring it down and give you a twirl too, Martin?"

Nonna's joke fell flat on two counts. First, she got Dad's name wrong (for the millionth time) and secondly. . .

"Mum! Was *that* where you were this morning?" my mum blurted out. "Did you deliberately go back to the shopping centre and buy the dress and jacket that Joan liked too?!"

For half a second, Nonna looked as if she was on the verge of realizing how mean that was. Then she put on her best defiant expression and gave a careless shrug (which nearly dislodged the teetering mound of scarlet towel wound round her head).

"Well, I couldn't *help* it, Nicola, dear!"

"You *could* help it!" snapped Mum. "When we left that shop, I had you *both* agreeing to a rule; and in case you've forgotten, it was that you and Joan were going to forget about that particular outfit and buy something else entirely. And that was *fair*, Mum!"

"Ha! Well, all's fair in love and fashion!" Nonna

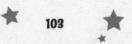

trilled in a tinkly voice, as if Mum's indignant statement was the silliest thing she'd ever heard. "Excuse me – I'm off to make myself useful and get a load of laundry on. . ."

There – that was practically an admission of guilt. Like I said, Nonna *never* did any housework, so if she was offering to do some clothes washing, it was because she felt bad (with knobs on).

"Hey . . . is she driving you crazy?" Dad asked Mum softly, as Nonna breezed towards the kitchen.

"*Beyond* crazy," Mum sighed, slightly tearfully, with a rueful little smile on her face.

Dad stepped forward and gave her an I-understand hug. And, of course, he really *did* understand; he'd had years of being Nonna's son-in-law.

"Hellooooo!" came a sudden shout, after a clunk of the front door opening.

"AAAA-EEEEEE-OOOOO!" came another shout.

Dad sprang back from the hug the instant we all heard Will and Martha's calls. Mum hurriedly dropped her dress behind the armchair, so her soon-to-be second husband wouldn't get an unlucky glimpse of it.

"Will!" Dad called out, a bit too jovially. "Surprise! I've moved back into my old room!!"

Will's face appeared in the doorway, smiling but slightly ashen. He was really, *really* hoping that Dad was just joking, you could tell.

"Only joking!!" Dad laughed, excessively loudly.

"Cool! Ha ha ha!!" Will laughed back, relieved.

"Guess what?" Mum said next, to Will, as she held her arms out to take a happily drooling Martha from him. "Me and Max are officially divorced!"

"Cool!" Will repeated, now *extra* relieved.

Well, I could have stayed there all day and watched this strange scene of awkward smiles between exes and future husbands and wives, but I'd *just* thought of something slightly crucial. . .

"Back in a second," I muttered, though I didn't suppose anyone was listening.

The something I'd just thought of: since Nonna never used the washing machine, I worried that she'd be putting all the laundry – including my best jeans – in the oven.

But no . . . she wasn't *quite* that mad.

"Ah, Sadie, sweetheart!" Nonna turned to smile at me as she pushed the large on button that she couldn't mistake on the non-oven washing machine. "How about making your nonna a nice cup of tea?"

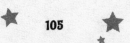

"NO!!!" I yelled at the top of my voice.

That wasn't because I deeply resented the idea of making her a cup of tea (yet again), or that *I'd* gone mad.

It was because I'd just seen a whiskered furry face in the glass of the washing machine door, looking very confused as the bubbly water began to rise. . .

10

When instincts go wrong

"Smile! It's meant to be fun!"

That's what Nonna had said to Sonny and Kennedy when they'd first fretted over the existence of The Twits last week.

It had been (unusually) good advice at the time.

Thank goodness she was too traumatized over nearly laundering Dog to death to repeat it when Sonny listened to the Chart Show on the radio this evening, and heard the devastating news that Benjii and his buddies had got the number-one slot with "Won't You Hold My Hand".

Anyway, that was earlier this evening.

Now it was midnight, and I hadn't been able to get to sleep. And not just because of the memory of Sonny's gutted face.

It was, of course, what had happened this afternoon. I just couldn't shake the image of Dog's pathetic face out of my head, as she began pawing at the glass door of the washing machine.

What got me was, *if* I hadn't wandered through to the kitchen when I did, Dog would definitely have drowned in a tangle of Nonna's undies (what an undignified death!), while Nonna blithely flicked through a magazine at the kitchen table, waiting for someone to scurry in and offer to make her a cup of tea.

But phew; Dog was fine. Hyper-clean, but fine. The Sunday emergency vet's bill *wasn't* so fine, but Mum and Will didn't seem to care about that, since we couldn't find the Fairy Liquitab that Nonna had put in with the laundry, and we needed to make sure Dog hadn't swallowed it and been poisoned by washing detergent.

Tonight, after she was home, safe, relatively unscathed and smelling of fresh meadows, I'd tried to get Dog to sleep in my room. I'd even bought this plug-in smelly thing from the vet's with my allowance that was meant to act like an anti-anxiety drug for pets . . . but Dog had hopped off my blow-up bed, crinkling across the bin-bag carpet and out of the door about an hour ago.

I just hoped she wasn't heading for the washing machine. Though I don't think *anyone* in our family would ever do the laundry again without checking the drum for a stupid cat who thought cold steel was something pleasant to sleep on.

At least Nonna was hugely upset and apologetic when it happened, which was the correct response, for once. (I just ignored the insane bit when she said she'd once heard that cats could withstand temperatures of up to sixty degrees, no problem.)

"Huh-a-huh-a-huh!" came a little plaintive cry, from somewhere down the hall from my Trash Pad.

Maybe little Martha had picked up on all the hysteria earlier and it had given her kiddy nightmares. (At the time, she'd just giggled when she saw Dog pawing at the glass as Dad and me tried to force the washing-machine door open.)

There were a few more minutes of "Huh-a-huh-a-huh"-ing followed by soft shushing, and then Mum gave up – I heard Martha's crying get a little louder, then the gentle thud of Mum's footsteps as they headed downstairs together.

Once the footsteps faded, I tried sleeping again.

Once I gave that up, I tried reading a bit.

Next, I doodled another fat angel on my wall in purple, sparkly gel pen.

Sigh. . .

It was no use – I was wide, *wide* awake and very, *very* fidgety. I pulled a too-small, cosy cardie off the clothes rail, yanked it on and made my way

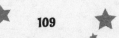

downstairs, to hang out with the other non-sleepers in my family.

"Mum?" I called out, but in a whisper.

There was no light on in the living room, and no sign of life – except for a small, dark shape on the floor, scratching behind its ear with a paddle-shaped shadow that had to be a foot.

Giving up on the living room, I walked along the hallway towards the kitchen, where I could see a beam of brightness peeking through the crack in the nearly closed door.

A thumping behind me alerted me to the fact that Clyde had decided to follow me, in case I was on my way to the fridge to empty the vegetable drawer of carrots or other sundry titbits.

The kettle was boiling madly, which was why Mum didn't hear me when I said hi. And she had her head in her hands, bent over a piece of paper on the kitchen table, which is why she didn't see me (and Clyde) come in.

Dog noticed me, though, and started purring from the comfort of the ironing pile, where she was happily shedding hairs over Nonna's freshly washed and dried knickers.

Martha saw me too, and looked up from the floor, where she was raiding the cat crunchies out of Dog's bowl.

"Aaa-eeeeee!" she cooed happily, with cat-crunchie crumbs round her rosebud mouth.

"Mum!" I called out in mild alarm. "Martha's eating cat food!"

After I scooped up my gurgling little sister, I was too busy prising crunchies out of her tight fist to notice Mum's face.

And then I saw.

I saw that she had been crying, and that big, fat tears had dribbled on to her copy of the divorce letter, swelling up random vowels and consonants with their wetness.

I also saw an old photo album opened beside her, with snaps of Mum in her puffy, fluffy white wedding dress, and Dad in the smart suit he'd never be able to fit into again.

"Oh, Sadie!" Mum sniffled, her face as puffy as the dress in the picture. "Why did it all go wrong for your dad and me? What would have happened if we'd stayed together?"

Mum might have thought she'd got it wrong, but I *definitely* had.

My instincts had been right about one of my parents being upset about the upcoming wedding.

I'd just got the *wrong* parent. . .

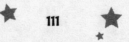

Mission Detract Claws

"Ho, ho, ho!" I muttered bleakly.

Lying on the ground, I stared up at the baubles dangling from the branches of the Christmas tree.

I hadn't checked with Mum, but I remembered her saying *last* Christmas that we could buy some new twinkly bits for this Christmas (which of course wasn't due for several months). So I'd figured she wouldn't mind me raiding the cardboard box in the attic for the tattiest of the trinkets and sticking them out here on my pet Christmas tree, in an effort to cheer myself up. (It wasn't working, by the way.)

Anyway, Mum wasn't likely to notice much of anything at the moment, going by her mood last night. . .

"I'm just in a bit of a muddle," she'd sniffled quickly, tidying away the photo album and the divorce letter. "I'm probably just tired, what with

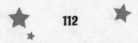

the wedding plans and your nonna . . . being here."

I think she'd *really* meant to say "What with your nonna being *impossible*", but opted for the more diplomatic option.

Then she'd. . .

a) stopped talking about "getting things wrong"
b) started telling me to ignore her silliness, as she was "just tired"
c) given Martha a rusk to eat instead of cat food, and
d) made us all hot chocolate (lukewarm and light on the chocolate for Martha)

because she knew that. . .

a) she'd scared me a bit
b) she'd scared me a *lot*, actually
c) cat food wasn't part of a baby's balanced diet, and
d) hot chocolate was meant to be soothing. (Ha, not in *this* case.)

And today?

Well, when I saw Mum this morning at breakfast, she was acting normal.

When I say acting, I *mean* acting; the smile wasn't very convincing and she was pretending to everyone that her red-rimmed eyes were due to a previously unknown allergic reaction to dust mites.

"It's the pets – I *know* it is. . ." Nonna had muttered darkly, over her morning cup of coffee (made by Will). She was frowning at Dog, even though she'd nearly drowned her last night, and Clyde, who was looking *extra*-cute with one ear flopped down as he weed in his litter tray.

I was quite glad at that point to know that Dog had chosen to shed a shedload of cat-hair over her undies in the middle of the night, and that Clyde had been found first thing this morning by Sonny, eating the corner out of Nonna's favourite handbag.

And now it was afternoon, and after school, and no one was home except me.

Mum was still at work (of course). There was a note from Will to say that he'd taken Martha to baby massage class (I pictured the babies doing the massage to the parents – much more tricky and surreal than the other way round).

There was also a note from Nonna, explaining that she'd gone to Borough Market in South London to look at the lovely antiques stalls there (pity she was muddling up Portobello Market with the one at Borough, where all she'd find was stuffed organic olives and hand-reared wild-boar sausages).

And Sonny? He was bound to still be in serious crisis talks with Benny and the band after school, in the light of the Great Twits-Hit-Number-One Disaster.

"Hey, Sadie!"

Or maybe he wasn't.

"What are you doing?" he asked, panting as he wriggled through the bent railings at the bottom of our garden to come join me in the mini-woods.

"I'm currently orbiting the moon," I said flatly, staying right where I was and gazing up at the purple, pink and silver baubles bobbing on the branches of the Christmas tree.

"Yeah, right!" mumbled Sonny, as he settled himself down beside me. "So, what's new?"

Well, I *could* have said, *Mum is regretting her decision to get married to Will, and maybe wants to get back with our dad.*

"Absolutely nothing," I said instead, thinking that the truth could blow his tiny mind.

"Well, the decorations are!" he said, pointing up to my handiwork.

"Whatever," I answered vaguely. The truth was,

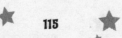

my tiny mind was a bit too blown for much idle chit-chat today.

"Want to know what's new with me?" he asked, putting his hands behind his head too.

"You've employed a crack team of ex-SAS soldiers to kidnap and neutralize every member of The Twits?" I suggested.

"I think Hal *did* try to get them, but they were doing a kids' party instead," Sonny joked back, sounding quite witty for once. "Anyway, get this! Our video's going to get shown on the BBC on Saturday morning, on the—"

He didn't need to tell me the name of the show – I already knew the name of the show. Everyone did. Which meant everyone at school would be watching it on Saturday morning. They'd all see me, in a dumb T-shirt with my name on it, being shoved along a pavement in a dumb office chair, with a dumb look of sheer panic on my face.

Arghhhhh . . . could today get any worse?

"Miaow!" miaowed Dog from somewhere or other.

"Can I see the video before Saturday?" I suddenly asked, thinking I'd rather prepare myself for the shame that was coming than watch it when I knew the entire population of my *school* was watching (and sniggering at) it.

"Uh-uh. I want to see it too, but Benny says it's not finished yet," said Sonny, picking up on my mild hysteria.

"Miaowwww!!"

"But isn't there a . . . what's it called? When it's not finished, but you can sort of get the idea? A 'rough cut', isn't it?" I suggested, ignoring Dog and whatever she was doing. (Probably picking the best vantage point for watching delicious small birds hopping around on the gravestones in the cemetery beyond.)

"It's not even at *that* stage," said Sonny. "Kennedy wasn't in school today – Richie the director called him in to do extra close-ups for his solo bits. After that, they'll be editing right up to the last minute, till it goes on air!"

"Hope it's not *too* much of a close-up. . ." I mumbled, thinking that there wasn't a TV widescreened enough to deal with that big plate face with a camera zoomed tightly in on it.

"Still, it's pretty cool, isn't it? Even if it *is* coming out a week after The Twist's video and single. But hopefully people will still—"

"MIAOWWWWWWWW-owww-owwww. . ."

There I was a couple of seconds ago, wondering how things could get any worse.

And now here came a cat, hurtling out of the

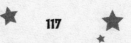

top of the Christmas tree, where it had climbed too high, trying and failing to catch on to every passing branch as it fell.

I could have been wrong, but it looked from here like the only thing that was going to break Dog's fall was either my or Sonny's face.

I only hoped there was an emergency "DETRACT CLAWS!" button on Dog somewhere that she could press before she landed. . .

The non-scientific experiment

"He's not really here. He's a figment of your imagination," Hannah tried to convince me, as I opened the front door.

"Hannah, he's *not* a figment of my imagination. He's hacking off the heads of my neighbour's roses with a retractable light-sabre!"

"HARRY! Put the light-sabre down NOW!!" Hannah barked.

Then she turned to me and fluttered her eyelashes sweetly.

"I didn't know I'd have to look after him after school today. Can I still come in?"

"Do you have a muzzle for your weasel?" I asked, staring dubiously at Harry.

"No, but I brought chocolate!" she said hopefully, holding out a giant, family-size bar of Galaxy as a bribe.

"Can he stay outside? Maybe in our old bike shed?" I suggested.

"It's not fair, but I think that's illegal," Hannah sighed, with a shrug. "But I really, *really* want to see your outfit for the wedding and your mum's too – *please*! We'll just stay for a minute. I'll tie him up or something. Just as long as it's nowhere neighbours can see and call Social Services."

"OK," I relented. What was the difference? My house was already full of visitors. Like. . .

- The entire band: who were holed up in Sonny's bedroom this Tuesday afternoon, supposedly having a post-mortem on the chart position of The Twits' single at the weekend – but they were last seen (when I came out of the loo) huddled round my brother as he took a call from their manager.
- Cormac: who'd arrived ten minutes ago, dropped off from a hearse after a funeral (*that* got Nonna frowning out of the front window), to give us a bunch of free tickets for his first-ever real comedy gig in a couple of days' time.
- Letty: she'd appeared just after Cormac did, with her little sister, Charonna, who was gripping a pink fairy autograph album (total number of autographs in it so far: none.

Though Charonna was hoping to change that once she saw Sonny and Co.).

- Gran: merrily bouncing Martha on her knee in the kitchen, singing old Irish folk songs out of tune and studiously blanking Nonna (yep, she'd heard about the treacherous purchase of the peppermint-green dress).
- Nonna: ignoring the fact that she was being blanked, Nonna was holed up in the living room, watching a rerun of *A Place In The Sun*, which happened to be in Spain this time round. (I'd just spotted her dabbing her eyes and muttering, "My *bella casa*! When will I see my *petit bella casa*!", merrily muddling up English, French and Spanish in one go.)

Then there was Will, who was on the computer, tensely checking on the exact delivery times of several something-or-others that were vital to the wedding reception we'd be having here in the house on Saturday.

Only Mum was missing, still hard at work trying to convince fourteen-year-old boys who liked Def Jam and death metal to get excited about Tchaikovsky and Beethoven. (Unless, of course, she was hiding in the staffroom toilets, crying about the wedding that was happening in four days' time. . .)

"Harry – get inside!" Hannah ordered her brother, ushering him in the door with a not-so-gentle shove before I thought better of it. "We are going to be here for FIVE minutes. And in those FIVE minutes, you're going to stay sitting on THAT stair, and play your DS Lite nicely. OK?"

"OK!" grunted Harry, giving Hannah a sarcastic salute.

"Come upstairs," I told Hannah, trudging upwards, towards the Trash Pad, where Cormac was sitting cross-legged on the floor in his funeral suit, signing an autograph for Charonna.

". . .so I was thinking that I might do something about pet cemeteries in my act on Thursday," we walked in to hear Cormac tell Letty as he scrawled.

Letty looked pleasantly interested. This time last week, the very idea of Cormac talking directly to her – and only her – would have had my best friend hyperventilating with excitement. What a difference a week and a switch of Fantasy Boyfriends makes. . .

"That sounds good!" Letty said encouragingly, while Charonna sighed happily at the sight of her

first-ever autograph. Even if it was scribbled by somebody that nobody had heard of (yet).

Cormac had already told me about his take on pet cemeteries – he'd shown me a magazine article about one before Letty arrived. It was called "Sweet Paws Pastures", and even though it had the word "pastures" in the name, its setting didn't look particularly restful and rural, since it was set under a flyover, close to a big industrial estate. There was a close-up photo of a headstone on the page, carved in the shape of a doe-eyed King Charles spaniel, and underneath was a gushy poem about *"a dear, true friend, miss you to the very end"* – called Splodge.

I could see that it was all a bit corny, and that if you were Cormac and had a job working with *people* who died, the idea of burying small dogs called Splodge didn't seem something to take very seriously.

"Don't think Sadie's too wild about it!" said Cormac, who obviously had picked up on my slight lack of enthusiasm earlier.

"Well, I guess it's 'cause of Dog," I said, pointing at my cat, who was sleepily getting up from the hairy indentation on my duvet, stretching out her long legs, and wandering off to find a quieter spot for part two of her snooze. "She's just had so many

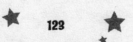

close calls over the years that I can't really laugh about that stuff."

In fact, as far as injury, illness and near-death experiences went, Dog had had a busy week. After all, there'd been. . .

a) headbutting the filing cabinet
b) falling off the wall
c) dabbling with cat flu
d) surviving drowning by washing machine, and
e) falling out of a Christmas tree while day-dreaming (probably).

The scratches weren't too bad, by the way. She'd landed on my neck, which I'd covered by draping a long, thin black scarf around it, otherwise I'd have looked like the latest victim of Jack the Ripper.

("Thank goodness she landed on *you*!" Sonny had said with great feeling yesterday afternoon, as he cuddled Dog and I'd gasped for breath. "I might have to do interviews next week, and I couldn't have my face wrecked for that!")

"Listen, Sadie," Hannah interrupted, acting anxious, "can you just show me the dress, quickly!"

"Why quickly?" Cormac asked, frowning.

"Harry's downstairs. Bad things could happen," Hannah answered darkly, tearing the wrapper off the chocolate and handing out great chunks of it.

"What – like he could *explode*?" Cormac joked.

"Oh no; that would be a *good* thing," said Hannah. "With Harry, you've got to expect the unexpected. So Sadie's got to show me her stuff *fast*."

I grabbed the hanger with the heather-purple shorty smock dress on it and was about to wrestle it off the rail when a great thundering and whooping came from outside the bedroom door.

Then *inside* the room poured five highly delirious boys.

"What?!" I yelped, as the Trash Pad was invaded by Sonny, Kennedy, Hal, Marcus and Ziggy, howling and twirling as if they were doing an interpretative version of an American Indian tribe's rain dance.

"Only the best news EVER!" Sonny virtually shouted in my face.

What? Crisps had been ordered to be handed out free daily to children under sixteen? Boy bands had been made illegal? Mum and Dad were going to get back together?

(That last thought made me feel sick. I couldn't imagine the thought of the house without nice,

kind, tidy Will in it. And if Mum and Will hadn't got together, there wouldn't have been *Martha*. . .)

"It's the best news EVER!" repeated Kennedy, the big-faced idiot.

"And it is. . .?" I ventured, hoping that one of these thirteen-year-old morons would stop being giddy enough to tell me (and the others) what was going on.

"They've only gone and split up, Sadie!" Sonny laughed in my face.

For a second, my blood ran cold, thinking he meant Mum and Will. Then I remembered that Mum was currently at work, while Will was on the computer downstairs, ordering biodegradable confetti.

"Well, not split *up*, exactly," said Marcus, a bit more soberly. Though I still didn't get what was going on.

"Benjii left The Twist to go solo!!" Ziggy squealed in a high-pitched burble, but it was enough to let the rest of us know what was happening.

"Our manager just called and told us! The Twist's record company announced it today!" Hal barked, looking round at me, Cormac, Hannah, Letty and Charonna as though we should start rejoicing too.

But all he got was a few "oh!"s, a couple of smiles, and a barely audible "Can you sign my book, please?" from a suddenly star-struck and shy Charonna.

"Isn't that great, Sadie!" said Sonny, grabbing my hands, like we were the best of twin-ly friends.

I was just about to tell him that was great but could he please let me go, when we all heard a blood-curdling yowl from somewhere downstairs(ish).

As one, all ten of us bundled out of the room.

"What?" said Harry, frozen in the middle of the staircase, with all of us glaring at him from the first-floor landing, and Will, Nonna, Gran, Martha and an irate Clyde staring up from the main hall below.

In his outstretched arms, held over the banister, was Dog, wearing the light-sabre (retracted) taped to her back with brown parcel tape (where had Harry found that?). I suspected it was meant to look like some rocket-blasting, futuristic space backpack.

"It's like a science experiment, OK?" Harry blustered on. "Cats can land on their feet from a really high altitude, *everyone* knows that!"

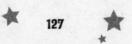

127

And I knew better than most, since Dog had landed on my neck from a great height, claws first, only the day before.

"HARRY! We are *so* going home, NOW!!" yelled Hannah, scooping a startled Dog out of her brother's hands before he could splat our cat on to the black and white floor tiles below.

As a puzzled and parcel-taped Dog was safely deposited in my arms, Hannah and her brother disappeared out of the house at top speed, as if I were chasing after them with a lit bunsen burner. (A reasonable idea in Harry's case.)

"It's a space-cat!" I heard Charonna giggle.

Yeah, and a space-cat that's just been weaselled, I thought, as I hugged Dog to me.

"That *boy!*" tsked Gran, closing the front door after him.

"Needs to be taught right from wrong!" muttered Nonna, in a rare moment of sisterhood with Gran.

"Poor Hannah. . ." said Letty, sounding as if she felt a sense of sisterhood towards Letty (for once).

Scritch-scratch, went a pencil, as Cormac wrote down a potential bit of comedy material for Thursday in a notebook.

"Yeah, but what about Benjii leaving The

Twist?!" Kennedy suddenly bellowed, getting back to what was important, in his big head anyway.

Pity the retractable light-sabre wasn't real, so I could vaporize the lead singer of Sadie's Socks. . .

13

Stare-offs and stressing

Clyde was hypnotizing Martha.

Or maybe Martha was hypnotizing Clyde.

Who knew the mysteries of the minds of the average small baby and stroppy bunny? All I *did* know was that they were staring silently at each other across the debris of breakfast on the kitchen table.

Maybe Clyde was trying to hypnotize Martha into giving him the cheese strings in the top drawer next to the fridge. (Paws made it hard to open the plastic, never mind the drawer.)

Or maybe Martha was trying to hypnotize Clyde into nudging the jar of jam over towards *her* side of the table (putting it within tiny-fist-dunking distance).

Will – scooping up toast-crumbed plates – stopped to watch them both in their bizarre stare-off, then gave me a grin. Which of course made me feel bad, knowing what I knew about Mum.

It was Wednesday now, a whole three days since I caught her crying over Dad and a mere three days till she (hopefully) married Will. And I hadn't managed to get her on her own *once* in our over-populated house, to see how she was doing. . .

Aside from the hypnotism, crumb-clearing and stressing out going on in the kitchen this breakfast time, a fight was brewing.

OK, so a fight hadn't so much *brewed* as started to bubble over.

"But *why* can't I?"

"Because you just can't!"

The first voice – the whiny one – belonged to my sixty-something-year-old Nonna.

The second voice – the weary one – belonged to Mum.

The reason Nonna was whining was because Will had to go and try on wedding suits this morning, and she was acting deeply *wronged* that Gran had come round to babysit Martha.

"Well, it feels to me that you're saying I'm not capable of looking after my own granddaughter!" Nonna grumbled, standing with her arms crossed at the head of the table.

I think the problem was more about *Gran* being chosen over *her*, rather than a huge, burning

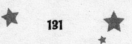

131

desire to hang out with Martha all morning. I mean, Nonna did like the peek-a-boo games and "this little piggy" stuff, but she always seemed to have very important phone calls to make to her Spanish builders or unmissable reruns of *A Place In The Sun* to watch when it came to changing nappies and dabbing away hiccupped, milky mini-sick.

"Oh, for goodness' sake!" Mum practically growled at Nonna, while she frowned and checked her work jacket for signs of baby drool and porridge fingerprints.

Thankfully, Mum didn't look like she'd been crying again (sorry, had that "*allergy*" problem again) but she'd definitely been a bit of a smile-free zone the last couple of days. Not to mention tetchy. I wondered if Will had noticed or if he just thought everything was "cool". . .?

"The thing is, Bunny," Will interjected now, using Nonna's favourite nickname in a bid to soothe her, "it's Baby Sing-Along Hour in the library this morning, and Joan has taken Martha there a few times already, so she knows the ropes."

"What 'ropes' are there to know?" asked Nonna, shooting Gran a resentful look.

Gran, meanwhile, sat in dignified silence,

dandling Martha on her knees and at the same time very pointedly flicking through a catalogue of pastel outfits, to demonstrate that she was *still* – at this late stage – trying to find a replacement for the peppermint dress she'd been denied.

Good *grief*.

I needed to finish my cereal and get out of this chaos. I couldn't think how Dog could sleep through it all, curled up there so neatly and snoozily in her basket, or how Martha and Clyde could concentrate on their stare-off. I should've done like Sonny and stuck my headphones on. Right now he was oblivious to the yabbering going on behind him, as he listened to his iPod and read the copy of *NME* he had spread open on the kitchen worktop. (He was listening to *himself*, by the way. Yep, as if having a single out on Friday and a video screened on telly on Saturday wasn't enough, Sonny seemed to feel the need to listen to the band's prospective album tracks on loop.)

"You know something, Nonna?" I suddenly ventured, hoping to help bring this argument to a quick end. "*I* took Martha to the sing-along thing once, in the holidays. And they expect you to do lots of stuff that you might not be into, like lying on the floor and joining in 'Sleeping Bunnies' with the rest of the mums and babies."

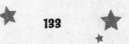

"But of *course* I'd enjoy doing . . . *that* sort of thing!" Nonna lied hesitantly, knowing that there was no *way* she'd risk getting her cream trousers and peachy bat-wing cardie dusty and grubby.

"No, you wouldn't," muttered Gran, ditching the dignified silence.

"*Excuse* me?" Nonna said with a pointed frown.

"*Well*, Muriel, face it: you're more interested in *clothes* than getting your hands dirty," said Gran, echoing my thoughts.

"Huh!" huffed Nonna. "Don't think I don't know what this is about, Joan! It's not *my* fault that you haven't found a mother-of-the-bride outfit yet!"

With that statement, Nonna got two things wrong:

a) it *was* her fault, and
b) technically, Gran was in need of a soon-to-be-ex-mother-in-law-of-the-bride outfit. (Did they have a specific section in department stores for that?)

"Don't worry about *me*," said Gran sniffily. "I'll probably just drag some old thing out of my wardrobe at home, since I don't suppose I'll get a chance to go shopping again, what with all the cooking and baking I'm doing for the wedding over the next few days."

"Oh, *Joan*!" Nonna laughed, in the tinkly, don't-be-ridiculous way that made Gran's cheeks redden up.

Uh-oh. An escalation in hostilities was seconds away.

Except Mum nipped it in the bud. She'd had enough.

"Look – just *leave* it, *both* of you. I've got to get to work and should have been out of here ten minutes ago," Mum said in an especially fearsome, no-nonsense voice I wasn't used to.

Yikes. OK, so she must use that same voice in her job at school or she wouldn't have got to be head of the music department. But at home, she was usually pretty dreamy, and said stuff like, "What was that, darling?" after you'd asked her three times if she'd seen your lunchbox anywhere or noticed Dog dangling off the garage roof by her claws.

Nonna stood with pursed lips, flustered at being told off by her own daughter. I noticed her glancing around, trying to fix on something to take away from the awkward silence and the embarrassment she was probably feeling.

Hmm. It was time to keep my head down, I reckoned.

"Sadie!"

Great. . .

"I *really* think you should put that rabbit down on the ground when we're eating. It shouldn't even be in the kitchen – it's not hygenic!"

Since it was Nonna doing the talking, I didn't suppose for a second that she was going to listen to any answer I gave, so I didn't bother pointing out that we were all finished with breakfast, actually.

I also didn't bother mentioning that Clyde was the most hygenic rabbit I knew. (*Yeah*, not that I knew many, *but. . .*) The thing was, our grouchy-but-beloved bunny enjoyed being groomed so much, and it was such a *nice* thing to do, that he got his fur brushed by everyone in the house every day – which equalled four brushings on a normal day, and five if Gran was visiting. Once Martha got past using a brush as a weapon, she'd probably make it six.

So between him having fur that never got a chance to shed, his habit of using his litter tray by the back door and his dislike of mud (he never stepped paw outside in the rain), he was an all-round clean machine. Cleaner than Sonny, that was for sure. When did Clyde last leave old food dishes and sweaty socks under his bed?

And here was the bottom line: if my soon-to-be-legal-stepdad, Will – a man with borderline obsessive-compulsive disorder – approved of him, Clyde *had* to be OK.

"What do you think, Will? Don't you think the pets carry germs and risk illness to your child?" Nonna wittered on, pointing now to poor peacefully sleeping Dog, who'd never done any harm to any human in her accident-prone life. (Well, apart from a few scratches to my neck the other day, when I acted as a soft landing.)

"Got to go," Mum muttered, choosing to ignore Nonna's sudden pet fixation.

She bent down to kiss Martha on the head. Then she blew a general kiss to everyone else (though probably not Nonna), and disappeared out into the hall, mumbling, "Where's my bag?"

"I'm going to go and help," I said, throwing a thumb over my shoulder in the direction of Mum's voice, and screeching my chair out from under the table.

As I stood up, I plonked Clyde on the floor, near Dog's basket. Maybe he could try hypnotizing her into never falling off stuff again.

Oops – with their mutual spell broken, Martha burst into indignant tears.

Still, it had to be done: trying to get Mum on

her own for a minute was like trying to eat crisps without crunching. *This* was my minute, and nothing was going to stop me from trying to talk to her, to figure out how she was feeling.

Except. . .

I froze, noticing something very, very strange.

Clyde wasn't just giving Dog a friendly sniff, like usual; he was patting at her head with his paw – as if he was trying to see if anyone was home.

"Dog?" I muttered, falling on to my knees (ouch) beside the basket.

If a systematic thumping on the head from Clyde wasn't enough to wake her, then. . .

"*Dog?!*" I said again, more urgently, as I reached out to stroke her warm, furry body.

Which was *cold*.

Oh, no. . .

The sludge of gloom

"'I licked his wiskas.'"

"What was that, Sadie, dear?" asked Nonna, frowning at me from her perch on the stripy picnic chair. The ground out here in the copse at the bottom of the garden was pretty uneven, with all the tree roots and everything, so she didn't look all that comfortable in her wobbly seat.

It probably didn't help that Dad had only *just* caught Gran as she nearly took a tumble off the stool brought out from the kitchen.

"'I licked his wiskas,'" I repeated.

Because my head was full of the sludge of gloom, I was finding it hard to translate the card Letitia had just handed me.

OK, so it wasn't so much a card as a piece of orange paper folded over.

"It's supposed to say, 'I liked his whiskers'," Letitia explained. "Charonna wasn't sure what to

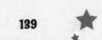

write inside, so I told her to think of something nice about Dog and put *that* down."

"It's a very sweet card," said Mum. She was sitting down on our old tartan rug, trying to stop Martha from grabbing the sweet peas from the jam jar on top of Dog's grave.

"And look – that's supposed to be Dog, as an angel," Letty explained, closing the card so I could check out the front and the felt-tipped blob with scrawled triangles sticking out of it. "The cotton wool is supposed to be clouds."

Letty's little sister had used maybe a *bit* too much glue for her cotton wool clouds – I had quite a lot of Pritt Stick and white fuzz on my fingers.

"I'm sorry Charonna got in a muddle and called her a 'he'," said Letty, referring to the message inside again.

"It's fine. Tell Charonna that it's really nice," I mumbled, pinning the card on the trunk of our pet Christmas tree, alongside a proper *With Sympathy. . .* card that Mrs Belcher our neighbour had put through, even though Dog broke the heads off her hydrangeas last week when she fell on them, and sometimes pooed in her garden.

There were other cards too: one from Cormac, which had a beautiful picture of a cat looking into a sunset; one from the vet ("Who'd have guessed that after all her dramatic scrapes, she'd just slip away in her sleep one night?"); and the most surprising one of all, a Spongebob Squarepants card with "Happy Birthday" crossed out and "Sorry your cat died" scribbled in its place.

"Harry bought it with his own pocket money," Hannah had explained, when I opened the card a few minutes ago. "He felt bad about taping his light-sabre to Dog's back the other day."

That happened on Tuesday after school; Harry was probably panicking that it caused Dog's heart attack in the night.

Or it might *not* have been a heart attack, exactly. When Will spoke to the vet yesterday morning, she guessed that Dog most probably had been born with some kind of weakness in her heart, one that was too small to spot. Which meant while she seemed quite fit and healthy, *kaboom!* – the little time bomb in her chest had been in danger of going off at any time.

Hopefully, it went off when Dog was in the middle of an excellent dream about leaping off the top of a tall building into a giant vat of tuna and blue tits.

Whatever, I was almost touched that Harry had been so thoughtful. (Though he could forget

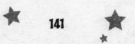

about ever asking for his light-sabre back. I was keeping that in payment for well, *everything*, including being hijacked by the whirly-wheeled office chair. . .)

"It's great the way people can be so nice when someone dies. . ." said Sonny, as he softly strummed his guitar. He was playing the theme tune to Disney's "Aristocats" very, very slowly. He'd originally come out here and started doing Eric Clapton's "Tears In Heaven" but when Dad saw me dissolving into sobs, he got Sonny to ditch it quick.

"I don't know about *that*," said Cormac, raising his red eyebrows. "When my granddad died, my Auntie Lisa asked if anyone minded her going to his house to pick out a couple of mementos to remember him by."

"But what's wrong with that?" asked Will, handing round a tray of tea and juice for everyone, though he had to bend a little so as not to be hit on the head by stray branches and baubles.

"Well, my dad caught her leaving Granddad's house with his DVD player and the keys to his Mini. . ."

I laughed a bit, along with everyone else, and it felt good. Since yesterday morning, the sludge of gloom had made me feel like I'd been walking around in a bodysuit filled with congealed soup.

But anyway, Sonny was right (even if Cormac's Aunt Lisa most definitely wasn't): people had been great. And here was my personal list of great:

1) Will. Will had been great, 'cause he'd had the sad job of burying Dog while me and Sonny trudged reluctantly off to our separate schools yesterday. And he'd been great because he'd chosen a spot for her out here under the pet Christmas tree – within miaowing distance of the cemetery – without me even suggesting it.

2) Cormac. He'd come up with the idea of the farewell party for Dog this afternoon, since we'd been too miserable to do anything but mope yesterday. And it was nice to have him here in his sombre suit, even though I knew he was wearing it more because of the comedy showcase he was going to straight after this rather than out of respect to Dog.

3) Mum. She'd got off early from work today for Dog's official send-off. (She didn't say, but I had the feeling she must have had to make up an emergency dental appointment or something; I don't think schools are too

keen on people skiving off for pet funerals.) She'd also let me raid most of the other non-tatty Christmas decorations to hang from the tree to make Dog's resting place more beautiful.

4) Nonna. She'd donated this really gorgeous red silk shawl with roses on it to bury Dog in (I had a feeling it was through guilt over the washing machine near-disaster as well as the general pet-moaning, and that she was slightly regretting it now, but you couldn't knock the gesture).

5) Gran. She'd been an expert at giving good hugs since yesterday morning, and I'd needed *loads* of those. Plus she'd made lots of very cute fairy cakes for the farewell party.

Actually, both my grandmothers practically deserved *medals* just for struggling to bend themselves double and limbo-ing through the bent railings to get out here this afternoon. . .

"Bit dry. . ." commented Nonna, taking a bite out of a pink-iced fairy cake.

"*Mum*. . ." growled *my* mum, low and threatening.

I didn't know if Gran had caught any of that; I

was staring at the recently dug mound, but I certainly didn't hear her snip any reply.

"Hey, why don't we do what Charonna did, and all say what we liked about Dog?" suggested Dad, holding up a mug of tea in salute to our dear, departed cat (and trying to distract the potentially feuding grannies at the same time, I'm sure). "*I'll* start! I liked it when you'd hold a finger out to her, and she used to touch the tip of it with her nose!"

"Oh, that was cute, wasn't it?" Mum said with a small smile. "And remember how she used to—"

I knew they were trying to be helpful, but I just couldn't handle that particular phrase; i.e., "she used to". It suddenly struck me that if I stuck around to hear any more reminiscing, there'd be more reminders of the fact that Dog "used to" do stuff that she'd never, *ever* be able to do any more.

Which is why I bolted, hitting my head on at least five baubles as I made my escape from the funeral. . .

I guess you can't expect to run away from your entire family plus best friends without someone following you to see if you're all right.

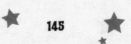

"I'm all right!" I barked from under my pillow, as I heard someone knock on the door.

I don't think they could've heard me, what with the pillow muffling my voice.

Next thing there was a rustle of bin-bag carpet as the door was opened and footsteps crinkled near me.

"Hey," said a voice, at the same time as someone sat on the edge of the blow-up bed I was lying on, which made me bob and wobble about.

"Go away, Sonny," I mumbled, wishing he could let me mourn in peace, instead of making me jiggle like a jelly.

Still, I was grudgingly impressed that he'd managed to knock on my door, for the first time in his life.

"I brought someone to see you," he carried on.

Great. It was probably Kennedy, who'd comfort me by telling fart gags and reminding me that I should go out and buy seventeen copies of the Sadie's Socks single when it was officially released tomorrow.

But it couldn't have been Kennedy – he wasn't small enough to fit on my tummy. And obnoxious as he was, he'd never bitten me before.

"Oh, Clyde!" I said softly, recognizing that familiar nip on my finger and coming out from under the pillow to give our lonesome rabbit a fond cuddle.

"The carrot and the lettuce still haven't been touched," Sonny told me.

Uh-oh. Since Dog had died, Clyde had taken up a couple of worrying new hobbies: not moving out of Dog's basket and going on a hunger strike.

"Come on, Clyde!" I muttered, pushing myself upright and giving this small, warm, *living* bundle a cuddle. He started sniffing at my lightly glued fingers and gave the cotton-wool wisps on them a tentative nibble.

"What're his favourite treats again? Maybe we should try and tempt him with something!" suggested Sonny.

Well, it certainly wasn't cotton wool. Clyde made a small gagging noise and spat a white wisp-ball out on to my T-shirt.

"Go and grab Nonna's handbag – he likes that!" I found myself joking, thinking of the chewed hole Nonna hadn't discovered yet.

The joking must have got Sonny thinking.

"Are you going to come to Cormac's show tonight?" he asked.

"How can I go out and laugh at stuff when Dog's just—"

I sort of choked on the "D" word for a few seconds, and finished off my sentence by scowling at Sonny for his insensitivity.

But when I caught sight of his face, I realized two things: first, that he'd only thought that the gig might cheer me up, and second, that a couple of fat tears were sliding down his cheeks.

"What?!" sniffed Sonny, wiping his eyes with the back of his hand. "She was my cat *too*, y'know!"

Wow. It's true that from time to time, I saw glimpses of human life inside my all-singing, all-dancing, all-smiling android of a brother, but I hadn't thought Dog's dying had affected him that much. I guess he'd been shocked yesterday morning when I'd found her curled up and cold, and a bit down since then, but I sort of thought that was the extent of it.

Maybe that was sort of *mean* of me. . .

"I, um, suppose I didn't think it would bother you so much," I told him.

"*Course* it's bothered me!" Sonny frowned, flopping back against the wall with my *Things I Wish Were Different* list scrawled on it.

(A list that was in major need of updating – in fact, I might as well rip that bit of paper off the wall and scrawl a new list that said *1. I wish Dog wasn't dead*, and 2. *I wish Mum didn't still love Dad. . .*)

"How did you think it's been, trying to pretend I'm OK in front of the lads in the band?" Sonny carried on, leaning over and grabbing a tissue from a nearby box and parping his nose. "I mean, all they care about is the *single* coming out tomorrow, and the *reviews* in the entertainment section of the newspapers, and the *video* being screened on Saturday morning. They're not really up for hearing, 'Woe is me! I'm gutted 'cause my cat died!'"

"What about Kennedy?" I asked, forgetting for a second that a boy best mate doesn't work in the same way as a girl best mate. *Girl* best mates are more dependable in the sympathy department, with hugs and kind texts and illegible cards from their kid sisters. In moments of crisis, *boy* best mates are more likely to punch you hard in the arm without looking at you and then make up an urgent errand their mum wants them to do.

"Kennedy just said 'That's *well* grim' when I told him yesterday, and then wanted to practise dance moves," Sonny told me, stretching an arm out to scratch Clyde behind the ear. "And I haven't even seen him at school today. I don't know what's going on – and he's not even answering my calls or texts."

We were both quiet for a minute or two after that. Maybe we both thinking the same things: about life without a cat called Dog; about a small, pining rabbit; about how much of a useless doughball Kennedy Watson was. . .

Well, maybe Sonny wasn't thinking that last bit; that was just *me*.

"Listen, can you do me a favour? Can you tell everyone that I just want to be on my own for a while?" I asked Sonny, realizing I needed a break from talking and thinking. "And can you tell Cormac I'm really, *really* sorry I can't come tonight?"

"Sure," said Sonny, getting up to go – and doing something so bizarre I'd have fallen over if I wasn't already sitting down on a wobbly blow-up bed.

He kissed me sweetly on the cheek.

I *know*.

I was still slightly reeling from the shock of it when I heard his booming, theatrically trained voice outside somewhere, calling out to everyone still at Dog's funeral that I was staying inside.

But by that time – thanks to inspiration from Charonna – I was engrossed in turning one of the little fat marker-pen angels behind my bed into

an angel *cat*, which happened to look a lot like Dog.

And beside my trainer pile, Clyde was happily nibbling the toe out of my second-best green Converse trainers.

(Phew, thank goodness he'd found his appetite again. . .)

15

Memories in *italics*

By Friday morning, my stomach had got fed up with two days of starvation and mutinied against my frazzled brain and my achy heart.

But unlike Clyde, the food I craved wasn't made of canvas and rubber; it was made of wheat. I was on my sixth Weetabix, to be precise.

Don't go thinking that just because I was eating the house out of breakfast cereal that the sludge of gloom had *completely* gone.

I mean, I was a *little* less wall-to-wall miserable, but it was hard for a girl to feel normal, when any second a pang that was as painful as a cat landing on your neck could pierce your chest.

And that was the problem. Every time my mind tried to drift on to anything that vaguely resembled ordinary, then *splat – something* would *somehow* remind me of Dog, leaping to the forefront of my mind in you-can't-ignore-me *italics*. Like. . .

- waking up this morning feeling all right, until I remembered that *Dog was still dead*.
- scrabbling for my favourite black cardie in a pile of clothes on the floor, only to find *Dog must have slept on it,* 'cause it was covered in cat hair.
- getting myself some breakfast in the kitchen, *where Dog died* – which is why I was having my Weetabix sitting on the bench in the sunshiny garden.
- wondering how Cormac had got on at his first proper gig last night, and then remembering that *he always mentioned Dog in his comedy routines*.
- thinking how important today was to Sonny since his single was coming out; i.e., "We Are Family". And now *Dog was gone from OUR family for ever*.
- realizing that the wedding was tomorrow, then stressing over the reception – people would be in the garden, laughing, *with Dog's grave just a few metres away*.
- worrying about how wobbly Mum was feeling, and then worrying that *I'd never stop feeling wobbly about Dog. . .*

Sigh.

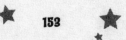

I tried to give myself a shake to dislodge negative cat-and-death thoughts from my head (and spilled splatters of milk on my school trousers while I was at it).

Once Sonny or Will was up and about, I'd check in with them about how Cormac had got on – I knew for sure that they had gone, along with Dad.

Hopefully the whole audience would have been as blown away as Martin Shore was when he caught Cormac's show in the park last Sunday morning. . .

"Hello, young lady!" boomed Nonna, appearing at the back door in the floor-length red and rust-orange kaftan she liked to sleep in. "I thought I was the only one up, till I felt the breeze from outside! Fancy making your nonna a nice cup of tea?"

I must have pulled a face without realizing it.

"Oh, no, no, no, Sadie, darling! What am I thinking of?! You just carry on with your breakfast!" she corrected herself, assuming – I think – that the face I was pulling was my weary, recently bereaved look, rather than my weary-of-you-Nonna-dearest look. (Guess which was nearer to the truth. . .?) "Now can you just remind me where Will and your mum keep the peppermint tea bags, hmm?"

Sighing, I stood up and followed her in.

"It's OK, Nonna, I'll do it," I said, clunking my bowl into the sink and flipping the kettle on.

"Oh, you *are* a love!" smiled Nonna, settling herself down comfortably on one of the kitchen chairs. "How are you feeling today? I did *worry* about you locking yourself away in your room all last night without anything to eat, sweetheart!"

I gave her a so-so shrug in reply. She could be quite kind, Nonna, when the mood took her.

"You know, last night, Sadie, I wished *so* much that there was something I could do to take away the sadness you were feeling, darling! I'd have given *anything* to cheer you up!!"

And generous too.

"I'm fine, thanks," I replied, breathing in the sharp, clear scent of peppermint from the box I'd opened, to stop myself from welling up again. "I just went to sleep really, really early."

"Of course. You were probably *exhausted*."

She was quiet for moment, which wasn't much like Nonna, and was pretty pleasant.

From other parts of the house I could hear the sounds of life: the rumble of the shower; the creak of floorboards; the happy squeals of Martha. No miaows or purrs, of course. . .

"And at least your ticket to the show didn't go

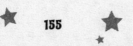

to waste," Nonna suddenly started up again. "Wait till I tell my friends in Spain that I went to a trendy comedy club in the West End!"

"You went to see Cormac?!" I said in surprise, setting the cup of tea in front of Nonna and sitting down in the chair next to her. "How was it? Did people like him? Did any of his family go?"

"Only his brother. . ." Nonna answered the last question first. "The one with the funny little beard. You know; it looks like he's stuck the pelt of a hamster on his chin!"

Oh, and of course Nonna could also be funny, when she wanted.

"Kyle!" I grinned at her. "No one else, then?"

I knew that Cormac was feeling a little wary about letting his parents and his oldest brother, Gerry, know about his comedy persona, since they worked in the family business and might not find it *too* hilarious to know that he made (gentle) jokes about his job and the subject of death.

"No, only Kyle was there," Nonna confirmed. "Though it's just as *well* that was all. Cormac was *terrible*! Just awful! He had hardly any jokes – just a few things about boy bands – and then he totally dried up. He was on and off the stage again in about a minute flat! Tsk, tsk, *tsk*. . ."

Ah, tactless Nonna was in town once again. But her clunky comments apart, my already-battered heart sunk for my friend.

"He must have had stage fright," I muttered, thinking that I should ask Sonny or Will for their take on what happened.

At least *they* wouldn't make it sound like poor Cormac might as well get himself – and his shame – nailed into one of the coffins in McConnell & Sons mortuary and never come out.

"By the way, Sadie. . ." whispered Nonna, suddenly leaning over towards me conspiratorially and giving me rather too much of a glimpse of her ample cleavage. "What's up with your mother? Has she said anything to you?"

My bruised heart pounded in my chest. What did Nonna mean? Did she suspect something? Did she know how Mum was feeling about the whole mess of Dad and Will and the wedding?

"No!" I lied, knowing I was probably flushing pink. "Like what?"

"She's just been a bit snippy with me, that's all. It's probably just tiredness, from trying to organize the wedding so quickly," muttered Nonna, straightening back up and gazing thoughtfully at the mug in her hands. "And of course *Joan* probably isn't helping, with all this palaver about having

nothing to wear. Actually, I'll bet Joan's attitude is what's got your mother all stressed and—"

"*Nonna!*" I blurted out, unable to stop myself as I listened to her blame anyone except for herself, as usual. "It's *you!*"

"It's me what?" Nonna frowned my way, unable to grasp what I was getting at, although it was as plain as the whiskers used to be *on Dog's face*.

"*You* are winding my mum up!!" I stated, feeling almost giddy at telling her the bald truth. "And you have been *so* unfair to Gran!"

I'd never spoken to Nonna that way before, but maybe Dog dying had just made me braver, somehow. Maybe life was just too short to put up with Nonna's bad behaviour.

Nonna, meanwhile, reared back in surprise, as if I'd slapped her in the face with a wet peppermint tea bag.

BING-BONG!

Seven-fifteen was a funny time to hear the doorbell, but it was a wonderful excuse for me to get away from Nonna, so she wouldn't see how much I'd got the wibbles from confronting her.

"Hi!" said Cormac, standing on my doorstep in his black suit, with a bundle of newspapers under his arm and a hearse idling at the roadside behind him.

A face smiled and a hand waved in my direction from the long, sleek black car, so I waved back, knowing it must be Cormac's dad or big brother.

"So how are you?" Cormac asked me.

("Since the cat funeral," he didn't add.)

"Pretty rubbish," I answered with a wonky smile. "How are you?"

("Since you flopped at your big-break gig?" I didn't add either.)

"Pretty rubbish," Cormac replied, with a matching wonky smile.

"What happened?"

Oops, I hadn't meant to ask that. I was pretty sure I'd just thought it in my head, till I heard the words out loud.

"I panicked," he said simply, with a shrug of his shoulders. "There was lots of my routine that I suddenly realized I couldn't do."

"Like what?" I frowned at him.

"Well, I couldn't −" he dropped his voice a little − "do the stuff about your nonna, 'cause I looked out into the audience, and there she was!"

Oh, I could see his point. Still, he had a *ton* of other material.

"And I couldn't do. . ." He dried up, just like he must have on stage last night.

"*What* couldn't you do?" I prompted him.

"Well, *everything*. My new gags about pet cemeteries, and the older stories about . . . about the party where Dog got her tail set on fire, and how I have a nuts friend who called her cat Dog in the first place. . . I didn't want to do any of them any more. They just weren't funny, not when I was standing on that stage, thinking of you at home and miserable."

Wow. He'd messed up for *our* sake.

I gulped, thinking how kind this funny, gawky, tall boy was, especially compared to the mad, tactless old woman sitting in the kitchen.

"Do you want to come in?" I asked, suddenly remembering my manners.

"No – we've got to go pick up some flowers for a funeral first thing this morning," Cormac explained, nodding back towards the waiting hearse. "But I know Sonny was dying to find out if the band's single got reviewed in the papers, so I picked up a whole lot bunch from the newsagent's down the road."

"Oh, right! Thanks!" I said, taking the bundles from him. "And are there? Any reviews, I mean?"

"I had a quick flick, but didn't have time to check properly," Cormac answered, turning to go. "Though I did see one for Martin Shore's gig. No mention of me, thank goodness – I must have come on too early for the reviewer to catch. Or maybe he blinked and missed me!"

Good old Cormac, making a joke out of his worst nightmare.

"I'll get Sonny to phone you later and tell you what they said!" I called out after him.

I didn't realize that what I held under my arm was Sonny's worst nightmare too. . .

Whatever-itis

In precisely four hours, twenty-three minutes, Mum was going to be marrying someone she quite possibly didn't love. (Help.)

But *huge* as that was, I had to put it in the back of my mind for now, because in precisely *two* minutes, the Sadie's Socks video was going to get its first airing on national TV.

Hello me shrieking in a whirly-wheeled chair. Hello national *shame*. . .

"Ouch! That was my *hand* you just stood on!" a boy's voice yelped.

"Good – I was worried it was the rabbit. . ." said another boy's voice.

There were lots of voices chattering and lots of bodies crammed into our living room this Saturday morning. Our living room, which was awash in pretty, overlapping paper trails of white doves swooping from wall to wall and ceiling corner to ceiling corner for the occasion (of the wedding, I mean, not the music video being shown).

The voices and bodies added up to fifteen nervous people made up of my family, *except Dog* (OK, I was going to have to try to stop myself doing that so much); Sonny and his bandmates (with the exception of Kennedy, who was sick); as well as Cormac, Hannah, Letitia and Charonna (who'd come along and got all the boys and Cormac to sign her autograph book *again*, plus asked them to write their favourite colour and flavour of crisps alongside).

So here we were, all impatiently waiting.

Most of my family just looked bizarre, in various stages of wedding readiness, except for Dad in his orange Hawaiian shirt, and Clyde in well-groomed fur (since neither of them were invited).

The boys in the band – they looked wired with nerves.

And no wonder, considering the reviews in the papers yesterday. With star ratings that ranged from two out of five to *zero* out of five (ouch), and comments like "cloying, sentimental piffle" and "perfect for anyone with a love-of-music bypass" and "bilge" (oof!), it made sense that the boys were nervy in general, and that Sonny had been hiding out under his pulled-down bowler hat for the last twenty-four hours or so.

"Can't believe Kennedy's missing this," mumbled Sonny from somewhere behind the hat, the equivalent of hiding behind a cushion during the scary scenes in a movie.

"Well, he's not exactly *missing* it, is he?" Hal pointed out. "He's just watching it at *his* house!"

"Hey, maybe he's texted that mad Mel to come round and watch it with him and his parents!" joked Ziggy.

Letitia's face fell, even further than it had fallen when she arrived round here earlier and found out that her Fantasy Boyfriend was a no-show.

"Yeah! She could make him honey and lemon for his sore throat!!" Marcus joined in.

I'd forgotten about Mel. So much had gone on since I saw her (twice) last Saturday that I almost wondered if I'd imagined her (both times).

"Now, boys, don't be so mean about your friend!" Nonna gently chastised them. "I'm sure Kennedy would rather *not* have meningitis!"

"It's *laryngitis*, Nonna!" Sonny corrected her, tipping his hat back for a millisecond to shoot her an amused glance.

"Well, they're *both* painful throat conditions,

Sonny, so let's not quibble!" said Nonna, arching her eyebrows at him.

It was hard to take her seriously when a) she got her facts so badly wrong, and b) huge, pink foam rollers bobbed on her head as she spoke.

By the way, Nonna hadn't mentioned a thing to me about my little outburst the day before – not one word. I didn't know if she thought I'd been rude, or *right*.

But between the recent death, imminent wedding and looming video embarrassment, I didn't have the energy to stress over what I'd said and how she might have felt about it.

"Drinks and snacks for everyone!" trilled Gran, putting a tray of tumblers and a couple of packets of biscuits on the table, attired in her finest towelling dressing gown.

"Um, just be kind of careful not to drop crumbs, please – got a party happening here later, remember!" Will called out nervously, as he paced back and forth with a grizzly Martha, who wasn't happy that her daddy had stopped her sucking on the lilac satin headband she was supposed to be wearing in a few short hours' time.

Mum was hovering in and out of the living-room doorway, busying herself with this, that and the other (fine, as long as "the other" didn't mean packing her bag while we weren't looking and running away from home and the wedding).

No – there she was, staring at the TV and biting nervously at her newly manicured nails. Was she nervous for Sonny, or herself? I worried and wondered.

Actually, did I just see her gaze down at *Dad* there? Yes, I *did*! *She* did, I mean. I mean, Dad had his head bowed, reading some text on the screen of his mobile phone, and Mum was staring *right* at him, her eyes burning a hole in the back of his head as if she was trying to read his thoughts. . .

Gulp.

And who, I wondered, was sending Dad a text? Of course, it could have been a client, chasing an order for Disney princess paper plates or Thomas the Tank Engine serviettes. Or Daryl and Kemal, checking if he was coming to the pub later, to catch the Arsenal match. But I couldn't shake the feeling that it might be his "girlfriend" *Angie*, saying hi, or maybe just checking to see if the band were all present and correct (minus Kennedy, of course), ready for their big moment.

"Who's the text from?" I leant over Hannah to ask him, burning up with curiosity.

"Eek! Must be only a minute to go!" I heard Letitia squeal on the other side of me, rallying at

the idea of seeing her crush on the TV right now, if not in the flesh.

"Um . . . just Angie," Dad answered me, slightly sheepishly.

Aha! I was right! It *was* her!

"She's, um, just said she's hoping the boys like the end product," Dad added, nodding at the phone.

Y'know, he didn't look like his usual laid-back self. Maybe he was on edge for the lads.

"Hey! I think the presenter's just about to introduce you!" Cormac called out.

There was a whole lot of shushing, as we watched the guy on the TV chatting in front of a live, bouncy audience and tried to catch what he was saying.

"*. . .for all you boy-band fans out there, here's a great new bunch of lads with their song, 'We Are Family'. Give it up for . . . Sadie Knocks!!*"

"ROCKS!!" yelled most, if not *all*, of the fifteen people in my living room.

Clyde dropped his ears back and looked annoyed with the racket.

"How could he get it wrong?" groaned Ziggy, while Marcus dropped his head in his hands.

"Don't they have autocue!!" moaned Hal, while Sonny pulled the bowler hat so low I wasn't sure

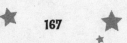

167

how he was going to see anything on the TV screen at all.

"Shhh!" ordered Nonna. "You'll miss your moment!"

"Specially *yours*!" giggled Hannah, nudging me in the side.

I bit my lip and shushed, just like Nonna said we should.

We all shushed.

We all watched.

We all recognized the corny song (though, admittedly, not *everyone* in the room might have agreed with me that it was corny).

We all recognized *bits* of the video, but quite a lot of it was a surprise.

". . .*Sonny*. . ."

". . .*Ziggy*. . ."

". . .*Marcus*. . ."

". . .*Hal*. . ."

"Why's Richie done that? It looks like we've totally copied The Twist's video!" exclaimed Hal, as each boy's name faded in and out on screen, as the camera came in for a close-up.

". . .*Kenideee*. . ."

"Whoa!" Sonny suddenly burst out. "'*Kenideee*'?! With *three* 'E's?!? Since when did he spell it like that?"

"And since when did we film *there*?" asked Marcus, confused, as the shot pulled back from Kennedy/Kenideee's big plate face and revealed a backdrop of the top of a multi-storey car park.

"Um, guys – Angie just told me to remind you that the director did do some extra filming earlier this week," Dad piped up, again holding his mobile aloft. "She said the edit might be a little different from what you might expect."

And here was something I, for one, *definitely* didn't expect.

As the camera pulled out further, you could see a grinning Kennedy/Kenideee spinning a girl in a whirly-wheeled chair around and around. The girl – wearing a red "Sadie Rocks" T-shirt – was laughing joyfully, her arms thrown wide.

The camera closed up on to her.

". . .the REAL Sadie!. . ."

Now, I don't mean to sound self-obsessed here, but I was pretty sure – one hundred per cent, in fact – that that *wasn't* me.

"Who is that lady? *I* don't remember that lady, Letty!" said Charonna, speaking for us all as Mel the mad fan smiled, waved and swayed along to the music in fan-ly adoration, while Kennedy/Kenideee rolled her around the empty car park in the dumb office chair.

"Has Richie cut you *out*?" Sonny said in shock, turning round to face me, though mostly I could just see his mouth and the tip of his nose under the hat.

"I guess so!" I muttered, not sure whether I was amazingly relieved or amazingly offended to have been replaced.

As I tried to decide which, I was vaguely aware of a jumble of boy-band boy voices yabbering madly, and the fact that on screen, Kennedy/Kenideee's plate face, and *his* face alone, was featured for the bulk of the three-minute film.

"This is *nuts*!"

"It's like he's a solo singer now and we're just the backing band!"

"Kennedy *must* have suggested that Mel to Richie! Why didn't he ask the rest of us if it was OK?"

"'Cause we'd have said 'no way!!'"

"Phone Benny! You got his mobile number? Did he know about this?"

"He *can't* have known about this!"

"Is *this* why Kennedy's been out of the picture for the last couple of days?"

"Do you think he's *faking* the laryngitis thing, so he doesn't have to face us?!"

"Oh, I'm sure he wouldn't do that!" Letty burst in, jumping to her Fantasy Boyfriend's defence.

"Dad – what did Angie say about this? Is she cool with it?" Sonny pointedly asked our dad.

"Um, no, not really. She got a viewing of it last night, and wasn't pleased with the direction Richie had taken it, but it was just too late to change it."

OK, so that's why he'd acted nervy. He knew Angie – and probably the rest of the record company – weren't thrilled with the video.

"Never mind, boys! All publicity is good publicity!" Nonna tried to say cheerfully. "Wait till everyone goes rushing to the shops after they see this; your single will go zooming up the charts tomorrow, I'll bet!"

"Shush! It's finishing!" Hannah called out. "The presenter guy will name-check you again, for sure!"

"Excellent, excellent! Did you like that?" the presenter said, turning around to a girl of about ten in the audience.

"Nah! They're not as good as The Twist!" she yelped into the mike.

It was as if all the air in the room got sucked out, and fifteen people (and a rabbit) instantly deflated.

"Biscuit, anyone?" asked Gran over-brightly, holding out a packet of HobNobs.

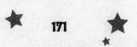

171

I didn't think anyone in the band would have much of an appetite for the foreseeable future. I didn't know how they'd muster up the enthusiasm to sing – as promised – at the reception this afternoon. If they managed to sing at all, even the most upbeat of stuff would end up sounding like some tragic ballad.

Still, every cloud has a silver lining.

And mine was that although I'd obviously been *so* awful at my part in the video that I'd been edited out of it, I could now safely hold my head up at school and NOT look like a complete muppet.

Yay! It was the best news I'd had for days.

Now about Mum and the problem of marrying the wrong bloke. . .

The significant something

The silky North Sea wave at the bottom of Mum's beautiful mauve-grey satin dress rippled elegantly behind her across the floor tiles of the ladies' loos in Islington Town Hall.

She was due to get hitched to Will here in five short minutes' time.

"Ooh, I *so* need to go!" she winced, clacking past me into a cubicle in her kitten heels.

Surreptitiously, I watched two women at the mirrors, touching up their make-up and chatting.

"He is *absolutely* gorgeous!" said one. "Did you notice the way he couldn't stop looking at me?"

"Stop it! You're awful!" giggled the other one, hitting the first playfully on her arm. "You've only been talking to him five minutes. You'll scare him away!!"

"You're just jealous!"

"I am *not*!" said the second woman. "Anyway,

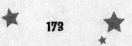

he's too young for me. And *you*, for that matter, Muriel!"

"Oh, Joan! Ted is only ten years younger than me! And that's the same age gap as Will and my Nicola! Isn't that right, Nicola, dear?"

Before you keel over in shock, yes, these two women *were* my grandmothers, and yes, they *were* getting on, unbelievably well, but the reason will shortly be revealed. . .

"Yes, Mum," came a voice from inside the cubicle, along with lots of rustling and some dubious breathlessness.

Will's poor dad, Ted, had come to the town hall straight from the station. He'd been nervous about his train up from Cornwall running late, and arrived anxious and flustered. He visibly relaxed when he saw our gathered group in the foyer, and relaxed even more when Nonna and Gran started chatting to him. Or chatting him *up*, more like.

"I just worry that you've got your sights set on wedding number *four*!" Gran joked, straightening the cream rose sprig pinned to her bolero jacket.

"Hmm, I'm not sure I'd be up for being a *farmer's* wife, dear!" Nonna guffawed. "Still, tell you what — *you* can be my bridesmaid if it happens!"

Nonna and Gran both dissolved into girlish giggles.

I gazed at the two of them in the big mirror above the sinks, in their matching peppermint dresses: Mum's sixty-something bridesmaids.

Oh, yes, I'd been replaced for the *second* time in one day, but I was pretty pleased this time too.

And who'd have guessed? It turned out that *I* was responsible for the change in plan, even though I didn't know it. . .

"Sadie, Sonny, your mum and I have got something to show you, and something to *ask* you," Will had said two hours ago, once the Saturday-morning TV-watching throng had left our house, and we'd all begun getting ready in earnest.

Me and my brother had the least primping to do, so were entertaining Martha on the floor with a selection of nursery rhymes (with amended, slightly rude words) when Will spoke.

Sonny hadn't been part of last Saturday's shopping drama, so his jaw didn't drop quite as far as mine when Nonna (size 16) and Gran (size 12) presented themselves in the living-room doorway, tittering in unison and clutching dainty cream bouquets.

"How – how did this happen?" I gasped, with my gasp translating as. . .

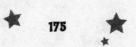

a) how had Gran and Nonna ended up in the same outfit, and

b) how come they seemed to find it funny?

"Let me look at you, Sadie, darling," said Nonna now, pulling me towards the mirror in the town hall loos, in-between herself and Gran. "Isn't she beautiful, Joan?"

Wow, that was new. No "but" added on at the end?

"Beautiful," Gran agreed, tucking a stray wisp of hair off my face and tidying it behind my ear (I'd ruffle that straight out again, as soon as I could).

"Thank *goodness* for the concealer on those scratches on your neck," added Nonna, finding *something* to pick on, true to form. "Anyway, never mind that. Here we all are, happy as can be, and it's all because of *you*, Sadie!"

All because of me losing my temper with her yesterday morning, apparently.

After I'd barked at her, Nonna had gone off and sulked. Then moped. Then mulled. Then realized (shock!) that I had a point.

After that, she'd disappeared off to the N1 centre, and bought the peppermint dress and jacket in Gran's size.

Back home, an unsuspecting Gran had taken

over our kitchen as her catering headquarters (I'd been glad to get to school when I saw the military operation taking place).

She'd been completely taken aback when Nonna had presented her with the posh carrier bag, and informed Gran that *she* was going to switch and wear something different.

Gran had been surprised, and touched. Then she'd stewed on it a while (for hours), and at some point this morning, in the muddle after the Sadie "Knocks" video calamity, Gran had confided in Will, saying how bad she felt about Nonna not wearing the outfit she'd loved so much.

So Will got thinking. He talked to Mum. They *both* talked to Nonna and Gran. They flattered them into trying their dresses on together, split my bridesmaid's bouquet into two smaller bouquets, and presented both grandmothers as an irresistible package to me and Sonny.

"So me and your mum were thinking," Will had continued this morning with the grans excitedly grinning in front of us, "that *maybe* we could do something fun. I know it's last-minute, but I thought maybe Nonna and Gran could be the bridesmaids instead of you and Martha, Sadie; and I'll ask my dad to be best man instead of you, Sonny, if that's OK?"

"Absolutely!" Sonny and I said in unison, as if we were the sort of twins who were always in sync and finished each other's sentences.

What did we care about the fancy, grown-up bit? It was a tiny wedding, and we were just happy if Mum and Will were. (Yeah, though I guess that wasn't a given in my Mum's case, worryingly.)

"Right," Nonna said now, "we'd better not leave the boys and Martha on their own too long! Don't forget there's a lovely man out here who's expecting to marry you in . . . three minutes' time, Nicola, darling!!"

"Yep!" came Mum's clipped response from behind the cubicle door.

As soon as Nonna and Gran left, in a waft of perfume and chattering, the loos went very quiet, apart from the rustling and the breathlessness.

"Are you OK?" I called out, panicking that Mum was hyperventilating in there.

"*No!*" panted Mum, opening the door and ushering me in.

She looked terrible; flushed and worried, with clenched teeth. She had handfuls of dress in her fists and seemed to want to tear the whole lot *off*.

This was bad.

I squeezed myself in and shut the door behind me, my heart pounding. I was brave yesterday

178

when I was brutally honest with Nonna, and it had paid off. Now maybe I needed to be brutally honest again.

"Look, you don't *have* to go through with this, Mum! The wedding, I mean! I know it'll be terrible, and I can't bear to think about it, but if you think you still love Dad—"

"What?" gasped Mum, bent double, wriggling and panting. "I don't *want* to cancel the wedding! Why would I do that?!"

"Well, what's wrong with you, then?" I asked, checking out the state she was in.

"My zip's stuck and I can't take my dress *down*, and it's so fitted and tight over my hips that I can't wriggle it *up*. And I need a wee really *badly* or there really will be no wedding!!"

OK, so I still didn't totally get everything, but I sure understood desperation when I saw it.

"Hold on – I'll try and ease *this* side if you do *that* one. . ." I instructed her, grabbing handfuls of petrol satin and yanking. (I had no idea that looking so graceful and elegant could be so undignified.)

A few seconds later, a much more relieved-looking Mum was sitting in front of me (on the loo, though she'd probably be *mortified* to know I'd said that).

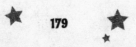

"So start again, Sadie . . . *why* did you think I'd want to cancel the wedding? And why did you think I was still in love with your dad?" she asked, gazing up at me. The tiara in her loosely coiled hair sat a little squint after all the recent exertion.

"Well, 'cause last Sunday – or the early hours of Monday or whatever – you were in the kitchen, crying over your divorce papers and your old wedding album," I reminded her, though I was surprised she needed reminding. "You said a couple of things like, 'Why did it all go wrong for your dad and me?' and 'What would have happened if we'd stayed together?'"

"Oh, Sadie – it was so late, and I was just tired and nostalgic that night! I thought I sort of explained it all, when we sat having our hot chocolate together after!"

Yeah, I *got* that, but I hadn't quite been convinced that she'd meant it. Not from what I'd seen of her behaviour this week.

"And even when I *was* in that mood that night," Mum started up again, "I knew the answer to 'What would have happened if we'd stayed together?'. . . Your dad and I would have driven each other crazy!"

Actually, they would have. My bumbling, music-obsessed dad was funny and great, but I remembered

him always winding Mum up. Whereas thoughtful, lovely Will put Mum and everyone first all the time. Hey, he'd even helped transform two grouchy grandmas into beautiful(ish) bridesmaids. . .

"But – but then you've been kind of jumpy all week too," I protested, helping Mum stand up and wriggle the tight material back into place.

"Well, that's partly to do with the stress of getting everything together for the wedding, *and* having to deal with my mother. *That* isn't easy, as you know, Sadie. Then, of course, there was poor, darling Dog. . ."

I gulped.

But I wasn't to be distracted; I needed to sort this weird situation out (in my head, at least). I remembered *one* more significant something I'd seen today.

"You were staring at Dad this morning – I saw you when we were all in the living room, waiting for the video to come on the TV!"

Mum flushed, blinked, and tried to think what I meant.

"Honey," she suddenly burst out, laughing. "I just noticed that Max was getting a bald spot!"

So was *that* why Dad was affecting a quiff? He was trying to grow his hair longer to hide a hairless, shiny spot that was appearing?!

"Oh, Sadie! I can't bear that you've been thinking all these mad thoughts all week and getting yourself in a complete pickle!" said Mum, wrapping her arms around me.

It was a lovely, warm, deliciously comforting moment.

It was only *slightly* spoiled by the fact that in the middle of that hug, over Mum's shoulder, I spotted the rippling wave of material from the bottom of her dress swirl round in the circling flush of water in the loo.

Oops.

Now how were we going to get *that* under the hand dryer out by the sinks. . .?

18

Amazing, yet possibly *terrible*. . .

BOINK!!

It was the first day of the summer holidays and Cormac had just thunked his head against one of the dangling Christmas baubles.

BOINK-BOINK-BOINK-tinkle-tinkle-tinkle. . .

"Oops, sorry!" he said, realizing that his practise high-kick had collided with more low-slung baubles.

"No – you got it wrong, Cormac," Sonny called down from the top of the stepladder. "It's neck slide to the *left*, neck slide to the *right*, spin, *then* kick."

Sonny was getting carried away with decorating the Christmas tree; he'd decided to recycle the paper-dove chains from the wedding last month and was wending them around the higher branches with great care, while Letitia helped out by holding the ladder steady.

I didn't bother pointing out to Sonny that with the first heavy shower of rain, the paper doves

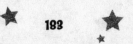

would turn to mush and it'd look like we'd draped our tree in soggy toilet paper.

I also didn't point out that Letty was staring at him with that familiar, lovelorn glint in her eye (well, she needed a new Fantasy Boyfriend since Kennedy turned traitor and broke her heart).

"Look, it doesn't *matter* if Cormac gets the dance routine wrong," I pointed out to my brother. "He's just playing a character in a boy band – he isn't actually auditioning to be in one for *real*!"

Cormac, dressed in chunky trainers, baggy skater shorts, and a tight T-shirt and baseball cap, grinned a thank-you at me. He had a first-on try-out tonight at a small comedy venue in North London (Martin Shore had passed his name on). He'd be unleashing "Kormakk" on to an unsuspecting audience, a big-headed, clueless, wannabe star and member of – yep – a boy band.

Me, Sonny, Hannah and Letty had had a preview of it already, of course, last Sunday morning at the park. Someone in the crowd that slowly gathered did shout, "Where's the funeral suit?", but since Cormac ended up with plenty of laughs thanks to "Kormakk", he sure didn't regret dumping the old routines and starting from scratch.

By the way, Sonny was cool with it. It's not as

if he felt Cormac was taking the mickey out of something *he* did, since he didn't do it any more. Not since the record company dumped Sadie Rocks. The reason? Well, they *did* get into the charts with "We Are Family", but tragically, only as far as number 98.

And, of course, it hadn't helped that their lead singer had defected to The Twist, replacing "Benjii"...

The laryngitis "Kenideee" was supposed to be suffering from, the weekend their awful video got screened? It was just a cover-up for him being in meetings with "D'Wayne", "Jax", "Harley", "Tiger" and their management.

He wasn't the *only* one who'd defected. Hal (who'd started calling himself Alan again) said he spotted Mel dancing crazily in the audience when The Twist played a set on *T4* a couple of Sundays ago.

Hey, maybe she could play herself (instead of me) in The Twist's next video – i.e., play a mad stalker...

"Y'know, I really, *really* hated the songs we were doing, Sadie," Sonny admitted to me, once he got over the shock of his contract being terminated.

"Well, how could you sing them if you felt that way?" I'd asked.

Sonny had looked at me blankly. "'Cause I was acting, wasn't I?"

And so, freed up from being in the corniest band in the world, Sonny was back blaring the Foo Fighters from his room and having a go at writing his own songs. (They sounded OK, though I had to insist that he let me help with titles, since "Baby, I Love Your Teeth" and "A Furry Angel In Heaven" – a tribute to Dog – weren't likely to end up getting Sonny any further up the charts than the ill-fated "We Are Family".)

He was also back doing regular acting, with his stage school sending him to auditions for stuff like smiling kids in toothpaste ads or cheery boy chimney sweeps in the musical of *Mary Poppins*.

"Aww," grumped Hannah, hunkered down on the rough earth with a Saturday supplement TV guide in her hand.

"Aww, what?" I asked as I replaced the grotty dead freesias in the jam jar with newly picked stems of jasmine.

(Gran once said jasmine reminded her a little of cat wee, so I thought these would be particularly appropriate for Dog's grave today.)

"Well, there's a big photo here from this week's episode of *Casualty* and Sonny's not it!" Hannah moaned.

"It's 'cause he plays a dead body in it," Cormac reminded her. "Maybe they didn't think a corpse of a teenage boy would make a very good front cover for the TV section!"

Speaking of dead things, I'd got on a lot better with Sonny since Dog had died. Somehow seeing him crying that day made me realize that unlike the Tin Man in *The Wizard of* Oz, he really did have a heart. (Though I was pretty sure that just like the Scarecrow, he was still short of a *brain*.)

"Hey, Sadie!" a very alive voice called out, all of a sudden. "And Sonny! Are you *there*?"

"AAAAADDDDD-EEEEEEEE!! UNNNY!!" an echoing, much younger voice yelled out too.

"Hi, Mum! Hi, Martha!" I called back, ducking so that I got a reasonable view of them through the shrubbery. "What's up? Is it time?"

"Yes, it's *time*." Mum nodded sombrely, though a delighted smile was playing at the corners of her mouth. . .

We were all in the hall, ready to say our goodbyes.

"Darling, don't cry. *Please* don't cry," said Nonna, holding my face between her hands so that my mouth squashed together like a goldfish.

"I won't," I mumbled through my goldfish mouth, meaning every word.

"Ah, Nicola – I do love you, sweetheart," Nonna said next, letting go of my cheeks so she could move along the line to Mum.

"I know," Mum replied. "You don't need to say this now – I'm coming in the van with you to the airport, remember!"

Nonna had originally come to stay with us for two weeks, while her flat in Spain was having building work done on it. That was – *oops* – more than two months ago now.

When she'd arrived, Will had picked her and her two huge bags up from the airport in the car. She'd done a lot (like a *lot*) of shopping in the meantime, and there was no *way* that Nonna and her excess baggage were going to fit in our standard car now, which was why Dad had so kindly offered the use of his big white van.

(Dad had dumped Angie, by the way. He said it was too weird dating someone who'd helped dump his son's band. But it had got him back in the dating game, and he was now working himself up to asking out the hairdresser who was styling his hair into an ever-expanding quiff. Help. . .)

"Oh my goodness, Martin is *such* a sweetie for taking me to the airport!" sniffed Nonna.

"*Max* really doesn't mind." Mum smiled through gritted teeth. She shot a look over at Dad, standing

patiently on the doorstep. He was rolling his eyes and mouthing "It's fine!" at her.

Nonna wasn't even listening to Mum's correction – she'd already moved on to my brother.

"And here's my rising star! My Sonny, Sonny, Sonny! You know, I *knew* you had potential from the first moment I met you! You were only a tiny baby but you had this . . . this *energy* about you that. . ."

As Nonna droned on, Will was checking his watch. She still had to say her farewells to him, Martha and Joan (who was – shock! – dabbing at her eyes), and possibly Cormac, Hannah and Letty too, if she was in the mood. I could tell Will was figuring that Dad would be pretty tight for time, getting her to the airport before her check-in closed.

And Nonna *couldn't* miss that plane.

She could *not* end up back here in two hours' time, when we'd all got used to the peace and quiet again.

This called for drastic action. I was frantically racking my brain for speedy ways to curtail her endless rambling, when something happened.

"*Aaaaa-eeeeekkkkk!!*"

Nonna wasn't shrieking because Clyde had just

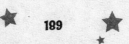

189

hopped and hidden himself behind her handbag on the floor. It was because of who'd come speeding along the length of the hall. . .

"HARRY!" I yelped, running forward to dislodge one little monster from Nonna's ample bosom.

In nought-point-three of a second, he'd scampered up her entire body, and had now tangled himself in the delicate cashmere of her jade green pashmina.

"You are *such* a naughty kitten!" I mumbled to him, as Nonna tsked and tried to extricate two paws' worth of tiny, sharp claws.

He was most definitely a naughty kitten, who'd managed to demolish a large part of the house since Nonna bought him for me and Sonny last week. It didn't take long for me to suggest the perfect name for him.

"There! Right, I better go, darlings!!" Nonna said hastily, now ultra-keen to go before she was used as a human cat scratcher again.

We gathered at the door to see her off – me holding Harry, and Sonny cuddling Clyde – as she retreated to the safety of Dad's van, blowing kisses all the way.

"Bye, everyone!" she trilled. "Love you all! 'Till e'r we meet again', as William Shakespoon once said!"

Ping!

It was as if I'd just received an email directly into my brain.

What *was* that?

Words; words that I'd definitely thought, but it was as if they'd been spoken by someone else. . .

On an instant hunch, I turned to look at Sonny, who turned to look at me. He grinned, with his eyebrows raised in surprise.

Wow! My twin brother understood, same as me, that we'd just had our first *ever* knowing-what-each-other's-thinking psychic moment!!

"*She's mad,*" he'd whispered directly into my brain.

This – this was amazing, and yet . . . possibly *terrible*.

Yes, I was getting on better with Sonny, but I hoped it didn't mean it was the start of him being able to rummage around in my thoughts without knocking.

Still . . . the lack of mental knocking *might* be worth it for the sheer enjoyment of winding Sonny up from a distance.

Time for a test. I noticed that his attention had flipped back to the van, as Dad started the engine and tooted a celebratory bye on the horn.

OK, so I'd try a quick experiment (while waving the van off) and send a message back. . .

I held my breath.

Nope, no reaction.

Sonny had no idea that Clyde had just started nibbling a hole in his favourite Nirvana T-shirt.

The big nerk.

Oops. In tandem with those *last* three words, Sonny's shoulder jerked a little, as if a butterfly had landed on it, or an unexpected thought was fluttering round his head, trying to attract his attention.

I smiled, realizing that this could *seriously* be fun. . .

Meet the sparkly-gorgeous Karen McCombie!

★ **Describe yourself in five words. . .**

Scottish, confident, shy, calm, ditzy.

★ **How did you become an author-girl?**

When I was eight, my teacher Miss Thomson told me I should write
a book one day. I forgot about that for (lots of) years, then when I was
working on teen mags, I scribbled a few short stories for them and
suddenly thought, "Hmmm, I'd love to try and write a book . . . can I?"

★ **Where do you write your books?**

In the loft room at the top of our house. I work v. hard 'cause I only have
a little bit of book-writing time – the rest of the day I'm making
Playdough dinosaurs or pretend "cafés" with my little daughter, Milly.

★ **What else do you get up to when you're not writing?**

Reading, watching DVDs, eating crisps, patting cats and belly dancing!

Want to know more. . .?

Join Karen's club NOW!

For behind-the-scenes gossip on Karen's very own blog, fab competitions and photogalleries, become a fan member now on:

www.karenmccombie.com

P.S. Don't forget to send your bezzie mate a gorge e-card once you've joined!

Karen says:

"It's sheeny and shiny, furry and er, funny in places! It's everything you could want from a website and a weeny bit more. . ."

Check out the rest of the
Sadie Rocks series

Sadie ROCKS!

HAPPINESS
AND ALL THAT STUFF

KAREN McCOMBIE

Sadie ROCKS!

IT'S ALL GOOD
(IN YOUR DREAMS)

KAREN McCOMBIE